GHOSTED CHRISTMAS PAST

TIS THE SEASON HOLIDAY COLLECTION

BRYCE OAKLEY

Edited by Lemon Wells

Cover Design by Lily Seabrooke

for the ones who feel like home

SYNOPSIS

L ast Christmas, I gave her my heart, but the very
next day…
Well, you know it goes.

MERRITT PERKINS HAS SPENT an entire year thinking maybe it was too cliche to be real. Dylan Camber: the cute private chef, and her: the nanny — connecting over being tucked away in the Rockies while working through the holidays. She thought they had something special, but immediately after parting, Dylan seemed to fall off the face of the earth. Not a single call, text, or even a DM for a year. Ghosted at Christmas, a fate worse than even Dickens could have imagined.

So maybe Merritt is a little extra icy this year when Dylan shows up to the holiday house again. And maybe she throws an outright tantrum when they have to share a bedroom. And maybe her entire head explodes when Dylan thinks they deserve a second chance at all the fun that they had last year.

It's going to be a long two weeks of resisting a truly irresistible woman.

CHAPTER 1

W hen Merritt saw Dylan in the kitchen like some kind of ghost of Christmas past, she immediately wanted to give the chef a piece of her mind— but she was holding the hand of an eight-year-old, so a proper greeting would have to wait. Instead, she pretended she hadn't seen Dylan standing at the refrigerator, her blonde hair tied into a top knot, revealing an undercut and the long lines of her neck.

"It's the chef lady," Huxley stage-whispered, tugging on her hand. His brow furrowed and Merritt could tell he was picking up on her tense shoulders, and the grimace on her face. What kind of example was she setting? She sighed as Dylan turned around, blinking at the pair of them.

"Oh, hey, Merritt," she said, one dimple popping out on her cheek as she smiled like she hadn't just completely disappeared for the past year. They'd been in the holiday house for less than three hours and already this Christmas was requiring a lot of patience and restraint. Merritt nodded in a stiff greeting as she took a deep, cleansing, calming breath through her nose. She needed to stifle the way Dylan's voice tickled down her spine when she said *Merritt,* slow and full, two syllables, instead of the rushed way of everyone else.

Merritt ushered Huxley onto a bar stool and opened the pantry door, checking out what kind of cracker selection had been stocked. She'd sent a list of snacks ahead of time for the housekeeper to grab for Hux before their arrival, but it took her a moment to find the box of crackers above her head. She stood on her tip-toes, fingers splayed as if that would somehow make her taller, cursing whatever giant person had arranged the pantry. What kind of monster organized a pantry this way? She sensed Dylan behind her before the woman spoke, the warmth of her nearness as she reached up, her sleeve of tattoos blocking Merritt's view and the good sense in her brain.

"I got you," she said, and Merritt could almost feel the whisper of Dylan's fingers against her back before she took a step away, putting the box on the counter. Merritt's skin tingled with memory and desperation as she tried to compose herself while examining a box of whole wheat pasta. She was being so embarrassing. Dylan had barely touched her and probably only did so by accident or to balance herself.

"Want some carrot sticks and hummus, too?" Dylan asked and Merritt turned to see Huxley nod. The chef murmured a quick "You got it," and before Merritt could tear herself away from the critical pasta studying, Dylan slid the snack onto the counter as if she'd prepared them earlier. *Had* she preemptively prepared Huxley a snack?

How dare she act all innocent and sweet. Their eyes met briefly and Merritt wondered if Dylan could see the flames of rage in her stare. Dylan's own expression was honeyed and soft, like she didn't spend the holidays last year in Merritt's bed every night, then never call or respond to a text ever again. Merritt had thought they'd shared something special, but then... then nothing. She ghosted. Particularly brutal. It took Merritt a month until she drank an entire bottle of The

Vanlaningham's least-favorite Pinot Noir and blocked Dylan's
number in a defiant attempt to be over her by Valentine's Day.
What was she even thinking? The private chef and the nanny
making it work long-distance? So cliche and unrealistic.
Better to just give her the silent treatment and get through the
next two weeks with her own feelings carefully unmaimed
this year.

But here they were again, one year later, at the same
holiday house in picturesque Snowy Springs, and she was
acting like none of the inbetween had ever happened. She'd
been dreading the holiday trip for months, secretly hoping
Julia and Kellen wouldn't be hiring Dylan again for the
season—she'd even thought about putting in a special request
for time off, but the pay this time of year was to die for, and
she needed the money.

She wondered briefly about the example she'd be setting
for Huxley if she threw one of the oranges from the decorative bowl on the counter at Dylan's head. She'd heard it said
that violence was never the answer, but maybe those people
just weren't asking the right questions.

"Let's go eat in the playroom and leave the chef lady to her
cooking," Merritt said to Huxley as she ruffled his red curls,
all decorative fruits still safely on display. For now.

As soon as they left the room, she felt like she could take a
deep breath again.They settled on the rug between the coffee
table and the nine foot Christmas tree, which was taking up
an inordinate amount of space for what was probably the
107th Christmas tree in the house. Seriously, did every room
need a Christmas tree? Or two? Rebekah, the housekeeper,
had really outdone herself this year with the decor. The house
felt like it belonged in Martha Stewart.

"You weren't very nice to the chef lady," Huxley said
quietly, staring down at the cracker he was loading with
bright pink beet hummus.

"I'm sorry about that, buddy," Merritt said, because what

else was there to say? *Sorry, man, when you hook up with someone that hot and they forget you exist the next day, it sucks to see them again.* That was the tame version and still not exactly appropriate. "We were friends last year and she hurt my feelings."

Huxley nodded sagely. "Onyx once hurt my feelings at school but I forgave him."

Merritt took a deep breath to avoid calling him a show off. "I remember that. You did great at that."

"It's not hard to forgive your friends if they're really your friends," Huxley said, like his eight years of experience on earth had given him the wisdom to give adults life advice.

Merritt knew he was being sweet and she was just being bitter, so she pressed her lips into a thin line as if she was actually considering what he was telling her. "You're so right. Did he apologize for hurting your feelings first?"

"No."

"You forgave him without an apology from him?" Was she nannying a tiny monk? In what world does a rich child, named *Huxley* for god's sake, have a straighter moral compass than most adults she knew?

"Yeah!" He beamed, his freckled cheeks and red mop of hair shining in the glow of the Christmas tree.

"You're so awesome," Merritt said, holding up a hand to high-five him. She had been his nanny for three years, and watching that little dude grow into a good person had been a major highlight of her life. She just hoped he stayed that way. It wasn't that his parents were bad people—she loved them like her own family, but they were Westchester elite: dedicated country club attendees and yacht club members, who owned a holiday house in Snowy Springs, Colorado. The type of people she had very little in common with, despite them being kind and friendly. She'd been with the Vanlaninghams since grad school, when Julia was her Child Psychology professor and asked if she could babysit one weekend.

She felt so loyal to the Vanlaninghams that she'd put off pursuing her PhD for years just because she couldn't figure out how to quit her job.

"Also Mom told me that Santa likes it when we are nice to people, so even though I'm pretty sure Mom and Dad are Santa, I'm going to try to stay on his Nice List." Huxley high-fived Merritt as she laughed in surprise, then he turned his gaze to the TV. "Mario Kart?" he asked. He was trying to cheer her up even though he always won. The kid was unnaturally good at video games for being eight.

"Sure." Merritt stuffed another cracker in her mouth as she reached for the two controllers in the media console.

She could hear Dylan in the kitchen, opening cupboards and turning on the stove as she hummed while preparing dinner. If it was anything like last year, everything she made was going to be delicious, but Merritt made a mental note to tell her it was a little bland, no matter what. 'Tis the season for forgiveness and Nice Lists, but she was just not feeling very festive, it seemed.

MERRITT HUGGED her sweater close as she walked the short path to the carriage house where she'd be staying for the trip. It meant a lot to her that the Vanlaninghams took into account her privacy and gave her a space of her own, like the bedroom and ensuite she had at their home. The winter air was brisk in Snowy Springs, biting at her cheeks, and her breath fogged in front of her.

Rebekah had told her the keycode to the door that afternoon and assured her the bathroom and kitchenette were stocked and ready for her. She glanced at the monitor on her phone—sure, Huxley was eight, but she still checked on his monitor after tucking him in, and kept it on the loudest volume possible in case he needed her in the night. She reached for the keypad, typing in the code without much thought.

Last year, Dylan and Merritt spent almost every night together in the carriage house. She pushed away the mental images that flooded her brain—fingertips on skin, lips on hip bones, those green eyes staring up from—no, Merritt was not thinking about that at all.

Her neck ached and she was plotting the luxurious bath she was about to take as she stepped inside, feeling a bit confused that all of the lights were already on. Did Rebekah set them to a timer? Maybe they were automatic?

She set down her bag and stepped out of her boots, instantly freezing at the sight of another pair already in the entry.

"Hello?" she called out, her voice low and half-hearted. She'd recognize those stupid Doc Martens anywhere. Ugly and non-slip and yet somehow still able to stir something up inside of her.

Dylan walked out from the bathroom in a loose t-shirt and low-slung sweatpants, drying her shoulder-length hair. Tiny droplets fell from her hair onto the shoulders of a threadbare white shirt, the fabric growing translucent against her soft cream skin, showing more tattoos beneath.

Merritt maintained strict eye contact in order to stay ignorant as to where else that fabric might have been growing see-through. "What are you doing here?"

"Hey," Dylan said, her voice casual like she often invaded the private quarters of others. Breaking and entering—a regular Tuesday night. "Rebekah told me this is where I'm staying."

"No," Merritt said, her head tilting in confusion and disbelief. "No, because this is where I'm staying."

Dylan blinked at her with the kind of agreeable expression one usually reserves for obvious statements. "Yeah, bud. There's two beds."

"There weren't two beds last year," Merritt protested, hurrying down the hallway.

"Yeah, I remember," Dylan said with an amused snort.

Rebekah had decorated more sparingly in the carriage house, with only a pencil-thin tree and a few holiday-scented candles. The kitchen was just off the entry, opening to a small living area in the back of the carriage house, complete with a couch and TV. A hallway jutted off to the side, leading to the one bedroom and ensuite. Merritt pushed open the door to the bedroom and was horrified to find that the king bed from last year had been replaced with two identically-decorated twin beds like some kind of 1950s TV show marital suite.

Dylan's suitcase was on the closest bed to the door, looking like a bomb went off inside of it. Seriously, did someone break in and search only her suitcase? Clothes spread from headboard to the edge of the floor, like she'd never heard of organization in her life.

Merritt's suitcases were lined neatly against the far wall.

"I figured I'd take the bed closest to the door in case of murderers," Dylan said, leaning on the doorway.

Merritt rolled her eyes. "And they say chivalry is dead."

"Alive and well. They are very wrong, indeed."

"You know who else is wrong? Rebekah. For thinking we should share a bedroom." Merritt turned on her heel and stomped back to the front door, pausing just long enough to slip her boots back on, then opened the door and let it slam closed behind her. Or, really, she'd have loved if it slammed, but the door probably cost more than the monthly rent of her first apartment back in the city, and it shut silently, clicking with finality back into place.

CHAPTER 2

DYLAN

Dylan was leaning against the headboard reading a book when Merritt stomped back in, her olive-toned cheeks reddened by the cold. Or rage. Or both? What was her deal? They'd had such a good time last Christmas, and although they hadn't connected over the past year, Dylan had been hoping they could pick up where they'd left off. However, someone apparently informed Merritt that Dylan had been caught stealing toys from needy children, because the woman obviously could not stand her anymore.

She was... confused, to say the least. And very, very wary. One year ago, they couldn't keep their hands off of each other, and now Dylan was trying to plot how to sleep with one eye open. She'd joked earlier about sleeping near the door in case of murderers, but what if the real murderer was in the bed three feet from her?

Maybe she just needed time. Dylan had an odd feeling that asking her what was wrong was not a wise move, because she seemed like one of those women that would then be even madder that Dylan didn't *already* know what was wrong.

Dylan stuck a thumb between the pages to hold her place and looked across the room to where Merritt was fighting a losing battle with her suitcase's zipper. Her dark hair was mussed, like she'd been raking her hands through her curls, and her full lips were turned down in a scowl. "Do you need help?" Dylan asked.

"No," Merritt snapped, smacking at the lock like percussive persuasion would solve the problem. "I don't need you or your help." Her curls fell into her face and she shoved them back with frustration.

Dylan grimaced, wondering if her eyebrows still existed or if they were a singed from the fire Merritt just breathed her way. She opened her book again, trying to drown out the absolutely feral noises Merritt was snarling across the room.

Maybe she should be the one begging Rebekah for a new sleeping arrangement. Last year, she'd been in one of the basement rooms, and she'd frozen every night to the point that Rebekah had given her four duvets. Four duvets and she still shivered every night.

Well, that was her on the nights she wasn't in the cozy as hell carriage house. She'd made one remark about how much better she liked this place and Rebekah must have thought she'd wanted the change. So, maybe this was a tiny bit her fault. That king bed that had been in the room before was super comfortable, but these beds were fine, too. Squeaky, but fine.

She'd pictured pushing them together when she'd first arrived, but now she was wondering if it was too cold to simply push hers out the back door and sleep on the back patio near the fire pit. At this point, maybe it'd be a better choice to lose a few toes or fingers to frostbite in order to not provoke whatever was making Merritt so mad.

She glanced over at Merritt to see her bracing herself on

her bed with one foot, putting her entire weight into trying to open the zipper. Merritt was a petite woman, and so that wasn't saying much. "Alright, this is painful," Dylan sighed, sliding a granola bar wrapper between the pages as a bookmark. "Step away."

Merritt glared at her, but didn't argue—for once that day—and Dylan took a peek at the zipper. It was just slightly off track, and with a few minor adjustments, it slid open. Dylan pulled the zipper through the rest of the track, quite impressed with herself, and Merritt was just starting to object with increased panic when the suitcase fell open.

Right on top of the suitcase tucked in a clear case was a rabbit-style vibrator, and laid out beside the vibrator were several lacy bralettes and panties.

Merritt flung herself on top of the suitcase contents to prevent Dylan from seeing even more. What more could be in there? Her interest: Piqued. "They must have searched it on the flight over," she said, not looking up at Dylan.

Dylan didn't even try to hide her smile. "Sure." Dylan walked back to her own bed and flopped down, resting her arm behind her head. Now she couldn't stop picturing Merritt in that lacy bra with the vibrator between her legs. She clamped her thighs together.

"This was supposed to be my own room," Merritt continued.

"Mmhmm."

"I was supposed to have this entire place to myself."

"I gathered that, yeah," Dylan said, pretending to be very interested in her book again.

"In a big bed."

"I remember. Fondly." She couldn't help herself.

Merritt scoffed and dug into her suitcase, muttering.

"What was that? I didn't catch that," Dylan asked, pitching her voice to angelic-levels of innocence.

Merritt's eyes rose to meet Dylan's stare and she could

nearly feel the daggers that began to fly through the air. "Just two weeks. This is only for two weeks."

For what it was worth, this was a pretty sweet gig for two weeks over the holidays. She got to stay at a gorgeous place in Snowy Springs, a cute mountain town obsessed with Christmas, and she had an excuse to keep busy instead of thinking about the family she hadn't talked to since her eighteenth birthday, over a dozen years ago. Sixteen? It threw her off that she'd avoided contact with her family for almost as long as she was around them in the first place. Throw in the years where she didn't remember being a baby and she was golden. She'd been her own person for longer than she was in that so-called family.

Still, the holidays and the sappy movies of happy families —hell, even the commercials—made her maudlin in a way that she'd rather not focus on. That was why the fun of last Christmas was so great. Merritt was the ultimate distraction. During the day and evening Dylan was elbow deep in some of the most lavish and gourmet meals she'd made all year and at night, she was feasting on something even better.

They'd left it on good terms, hadn't they? Dylan racked her brain to remember exactly how it'd gone. They'd kissed in the entry of the carriage house under some cheesy mistletoe she'd found in a storage closet of unused decorations, and they said they'd talk again soon.

Dylan had taken that to mean that texting Merritt immediately would be a little desperate. She'd give it some time. No way was Merritt giving up this nanny position—she was a perfect fit for the family. Bent over backwards for the parents, loved the kid, and flew under the radar. The husband was some kind of Wall Street guy, but Dylan didn't know a hedge fund from a... well, she had no idea what a hedge fund was in the first place, and thus, a comparison was somewhat moot.

Dylan watched the woman across the room tuck her

pajamas under her arm to get changed in the bathroom like it hadn't all been seen before, and Dylan took a deep breath. Maybe it was because she liked a challenge or maybe it was because Merritt remained one of the sexiest women she'd ever had the pleasure of pleasuring, but watching her kick the door closed behind her made Dylan certain.

She wanted to crack that shell. She wanted to see what would melt an iceberg like Merritt. Most of all, she wanted to make the most of the time they had together—to make Merritt see they were much better off spending the holiday having fun together rather than trading glares or whatever she thought they'd be doing in each other's vicinity. Two weeks could be a short amount of time or a long amount of time, depending on the motive.

Like any good chef, Dylan knew every recipe was simply a series of tasks. It was easy to get overwhelmed when looking at the 400 steps of a complete meal, breaking each section down to perfect timing.

Making Merritt warm up to her was exactly the same type of game plan. She just had to break down the entire thing into manageable tasks. The first task was to make Merritt remember that she actually liked her in the first place. If she went straight to reminding Merritt how good of a kisser she was or how she could do that one thing with her tongue, it'd scare her off. She had one cooking rule above all others: Mise en place. Everything in its proper order, prepared before jumping in.

Was it cheating that she already knew a bit about Merritt's favorite things? She'd say no, just for the purpose of the exercise. She picked up a chocolate croissant at the bakery that morning when she'd grocery shopped for lunch and dinner, leaving it on the kitchenette counter beside a fresh pot of coffee. What could she say? She played to win.

The Vanlaninghams didn't give her menus, so she was free to be creative with what she planned based on what was most fresh at the market each morning. Being in a mountain town in the middle of winter, creativity was a must. The way the pay broke down gave her a lot of leeway with sourcing ingredients, and she had made special notes of things that the family had been exceptionally excited about last year.

Dylan was standing over the sink peeling a large bucket of potatoes when Huxley came in, not looking up from his iPad. Perhaps he'd been lured by the mouthwatering scent of yeast and cinnamon.

"Good morning," Dylan said, wiping her damp, starchy hands on the towel tucked into her apron tie. "What do you want for breakfast? We've got fresh cinnamon rolls, or I can make a fruit parfait—"

"Cinnamon rolls are my favorite," he said with a hint of awe in his voice that made her internally high-five herself for writing down that fact.

"I remember," Dylan said, smiling.

Merritt walked into the kitchen, her dark curls piled high on her head in a messy bun and her chocolate brown eyes squinting. She shuffled in her slippers, muttering something about needing more coffee.

"Merbear, Dylan made me cinnamon rolls," Huxley exclaimed, holding up the sticky cinnamon roll as evidence.

Merbear. Dylan quickly ducked her head to keep from showing her amusement at that.

Merritt's eyes slid toward Dylan with deep suspicion. "Did she now?"

"There's enough for you, too," Dylan said, sliding a plate toward where Merritt leaned against the counter, filling a large mug with coffee.

"How thoughtful," Merritt said, glancing down at the plate. "I'm not hungry, though." She turned, leaning against the counter and sipping from her mug. "Yo, Hux, what do you say we go sledding today?"

"That sounds fun," Dylan said, suddenly feeling a bit lonely that she was going to be trapped in the kitchen working on a roast for most of the day.

Huxley tilted his head. "I wanted to go skiing. Sledding is for babies."

"Sledding is pretty fun, though. They have those giant tubes for sledding at the ski resort," Dylan offered.

"Maybe we could do that," Huxley agreed quickly, his mouth full of cinnamon roll.

Merritt sighed, rubbing at her dark chocolate eyes. She was probably annoyed that Dylan had such a genius idea and that Huxley was on board with it. "Okay, bud. Go get dressed." She glanced toward Dylan. "Can you pack us a lunch?"

Dylan shrugged. "Depends."

"On?"

Dylan smirked. "Are you going to ask me nicely?"

"Define 'nicely.'" Merritt tipped her mug up, gulping down the last of the coffee.

"A 'please' would help. And maybe agreeing to go grab dinner with me this week," Dylan said, definitely pushing her luck.

"Uncrustables it is," Merritt said, setting down her cup and walking toward the freezer.

Dylan rolled her eyes. "Fine. I'll make you something to take. No dinner, but you do have to say please."

Merritt paused, turning to face Dylan. She placed a hand on the white quartz counter, her stare darkening. "Pretty please," she growled. Or it might have been more of a grumble, but Dylan was an eternal optimist. Not exactly the kind of raspy begging she had been hoping to hear this holiday, but maybe there was still hope.

It was still early, and as she eyed Merritt in front of her, she knew with certainty that patience was her only way forward. *A lot* of patience.

CHAPTER 3

Merritt sat on the sofa in the carriage house, shoveling more mashed potatoes into her mouth—had Dylan put literal crack in these? They were seriously addictive. Creamy and lumpy and salty and delicious.

"Yo, Starch Queen, slow down," Ezra chided from the phone propped against a bottle of wine on the coffee table in front of her. The screen showed the faces of both of her best friends, Kylie and Ezra. Behind the phone, she'd put *White Christmas* silently on the TV so that she could multitask by chatting with her friends and pining over Rosemary Clooney.

"Seriously, I'm getting major chipmunk vibes with how much food you have in your cheeks right now," Kylie said, grimacing.

Merritt suppressed a laugh. "I can't help it," she said, mouth full of potato-y goodness.

Both Ezra and Kylie groaned loudly and dramatically.

She eyed her best friends, cuddled on a couch in Ezra's Astoria apartment, and felt suddenly homesick. "Are you guys going out? You look dressed up." Kylie's nearly translucent pale skin and dark hair stood out against a light blue crop top, and Ezra's burnt umber skin glowed with dewy highlighter and their bleached buzz cut looked extra styled.

They shook their heads. "You've just already forgotten how good looking we are," Kylie said, glancing over to Ezra, who grinned back at her.

"I could never. I love you far too much." Merritt paused to swallow her food and take a sip from her wine glass. "Aw, I miss you guys. I think it should be illegal for you to hang out without me."

"You've been there for four days, so you can't be that homesick," Kylie reminded her.

"I need on-my-side-Kylie, not sensible-Kylie right now." Merritt said, staring down into the massive bowl of potatoes in front of her. Dylan had made perfectly roasted harissa chicken thighs for dinner with a side of mashed potatoes— her absolute favorite meal.

She paused, glancing from the bowl to her phone screen, her eyes narrowing.

"Uh oh, Merritt finally realized it," Kylie said, pushing the long, dark curtain of her hair back over her shoulder.

"Realized what?" Ezra asked, shifting in the screen. They must have had their phone propped up, too, because Merritt could see that they were both sipping old fashioneds.

"That Dylan is trying to win her over with the love language of food," Kylie said.

Merritt swallowed, the potatoes turning to a hard lump in her stomach. "No."

"She just casually remembers the meal that you raved about last year? You wouldn't stop making that meal all year long. It was like 95 degrees and you were roasting chicken thighs at my place last July," Kylie said.

"Oh yeah, I remember begging her to just make a cold potato salad," Ezra said, a teasing grin quirking their mouth.

"It was my favorite meal *before* Dylan," Merritt protested.

Kylie widened her bright blue eyes, like what Merritt had said was patently untrue. "Maybe. Or maybe she asked what your favorite meal was last year, and you guys made it together and she showed you her secret to the perfect thighs—"

Ezra cut in with a laugh. "Yeah, she did."

Merritt gasped, trying not to show her amusement at the joke. "Stop that."

"No way. I'm naming my new erotic short story collection 'The Perfect Thighs.'" Ezra giggled again, leaning back on the couch.

Kylie rolled her eyes, patting Ezra's knee. "If a dumb name is what it takes for you to write anything new, be my guest."

"Hey," Ezra protested. "I'm working on it."

Merritt grinned, secretly relieved to have the spotlight off of her for even ten seconds. "Are you?" She teased. "What are you actually working on?"

"You can't just ask a writer how their project is going," Ezra protested. "It's bad luck."

Kylie nodded, her brow dipped low knowingly as Merritt laughed.

The door to the carriage house opened and Merritt remembered she had an alarmingly large bowl of mashed potatoes half-eaten in her lap. She couldn't be seen enjoying the same meal that she had told Dylan was "okay, but could use more acid" just hours before as she ate in the kitchen while Huxley was with his parents in the dining room.

Ezra and Kylie were still oblivious to the dramatic timing of the situation, bantering about Ezra's manuscript in progress as Merritt lifted a throw pillow on the small sofa and shoved her bowl behind it. She could sneak it to the kitchen when Dylan went to take her nightly shower.

"Wait, did you just—" Kylie started, but Merritt shook her head quickly.

"Hey, Mer," Dylan called out from the front entry as she walked past the kitchen to the living area.

Merritt cleared her throat and tried to make her tone unaffected. "Hey."

On her phone screen, Kylie's eyes widened and Ezra leaned forward.

"Is that Dylan?" Ezra said, a little too loudly for Merritt's taste. She grabbed the phone, hastily clicking the button to lower the volume.

Dylan tilted her head, watching Merritt. "Who's asking?"

"Her sexy, sexy lovers," Ezra called out loudly.

Dylan's eyes widened. "Wow, plural? You go, Merritt."

Oh, she was going to kill them. She forced a laugh. "They're joking. It's just my very annoying best friends."

"That's not what you said last night," Ezra called out again, and even Kylie was now hysterically laughing.

Her finger moved on its own accord, innocently slipping over the red end button. "Oh, whoops, I guess we lost our connection," she said flatly, putting her phone face down on the table.

"Oh, I love this movie," Dylan said, flopping down on the sofa beside her. She was always flopping. And now she was flopping right into the hidden mashed potatoes. Merritt tried to stop her, but it was too late. Dylan stiffened and made a few confused noises, while Merritt watched in horror as she turned around, lifting the pair of pillows that had shielded her starchy secret.

There were two ways this could go: Merritt could admit defeat and assume responsibility for carb loading the couch, or she could pretend she had no idea how that got there. Rationally, the first option was the best, but could she really choose defeat in a time like this? Obviously, she chose the latter.

"What'd you do this time?" she asked, clearing her throat.

"I must have forgotten this bowl of mashed potatoes

stuffed behind a cushion," Dylan said, raising an eyebrow as she held the bowl in one hand and a potato-laden throw pillow in the other.

Merritt fought to keep her expression calm. "Seems like an oversight on your part. You've made quite a mess."

Dylan pursed her lips, but didn't say another word about it. She placed the mashed potatoes on the table right in front of Merritt, then pulled the cover off of the throw pillow.

Merritt turned back to the television, unmuting it as the characters in the movie arrived at a Vermont ski resort with no snow. Well, Snowy Springs didn't have that problem, at least. She had to wear her snow boots just to make the fifteen foot trek to the main house.

Dylan pulled two parchment-wrapped cookies out of her pocket, placing them on the coffee table in front of the mashed potatoes in silence. Merritt eyed them carefully, but she knew a bribe when she saw one. Surprise nighttime cookies were definitely a bribe, and she was not ready to be on good terms with Dylan yet.

Still, she couldn't help but be overly aware of how close Dylan was, arm slung over the back of the couch, her ankle resting on her knee. Dylan's alabaster skin looked so light compared to the richness of her dark Mediterranean coloring. Dylan was mere inches away, and if Merritt paused for a moment, she could hear Dylan's breathing. Could nearly feel it on her neck again, warming her skin under Dylan's broad, soft lips. A sleeve of tattoos peeked out from under the raised cuff of Dylan's sweater, and Merritt glanced down at it, knowing exactly what part of the crow tattoo on her forearm she was seeing. She'd traced it with her fingers dozens of times a year ago. Had traced every inch of Dylan with her fingers.

She noticed Dylan's breath hitch, and her eyes flicked up to see Dylan's eyes set squarely on her, the intense green gaze boring into her. Slightly startled, she turned back quickly to the TV and cleared her throat. "Don't you just love Rosemary Clooney?"

"I've always been more of a Vera-Ellen fan," Dylan said casually as she pulled out her phone and typed something out as she smiled.

Ugh, she was probably texting some other girl. Merritt rolled her eyes. "Of course you are."

"What's that mean?"

"She's just so generically beautiful. She's like that typical beautiful, you know?" Merritt elaborated. "I think it takes real taste to prefer Rosemary."

Dylan didn't say anything, and when Merritt chanced a sideways look, she saw Dylan was still turned toward her, smiling. Ugh, that one fucking dimple. "I don't know. I think I have pretty good taste," she said finally, biting her lip.

What that sentence and lip bite did to her entire body, Merritt would take to the grave. She *knew* it was a line, and yet...

Her phone screen lit up with a notification from Huxley's monitor. Her heart stuttered as she reached for it and swiped open the app, taking a peek at the camera. Was something wrong? Sometimes Huxley had nightmares, and they were worse when the family traveled. Last summer in London he'd woken up screaming nearly every night.

When the camera screen opened, she saw that he was merely sitting in bed under his covers with a light. Probably reading. Still, she decided she'd better go check on him and see if she could get him to settle. He was an absolute terror if he didn't have enough sleep. Back in London when he'd had terrible nightmares and hadn't slept much, he'd had a meltdown so intensely during a car ride that the driver had pulled over and requested they get out early.

"Everything okay?" Dylan asked, interrupting the memory.

"I'd better go make sure," Merritt murmured, jumping on

any excuse to leave the room and the tension that always lingered between her and Dylan. She stood, grabbing the mashed potato pillow cover to rinse and toss into the laundry for Rebekah.

WHEN SHE ARRIVED at Huxley's room, he was sound asleep, the flashlight facing the wall and an open Goosebumps book on his chest. She'd given him her old collection for his birthday, and though they scared him a little, he was obsessed. She glanced at the title he'd chosen for the night—ah, Welcome to Camp Nightmare. A classic.

Julia and Kellen didn't love him reading the series, especially given his nightmares, but she found that his bad dreams were never about ghosts or haunted masks. No, his nightmares had always centered around being abandoned or forgotten somewhere. Yet another reason she was procrastinating applying for her PhD—between Julia's varying work and conference schedule and Kellen's absolutely soul-sucking work schedule, she had become somewhat of the only constant for Hux. The Vanlaninghams were fantastic parents, but she enjoyed the satisfaction of simply showing up every day for him.

She leaned over him to grab the flashlight and flip it off.

"Hi Merbear," Huxley said in the dark. She hadn't realized he'd woken up, and judging by his sleepy voice, he wasn't very awake yet.

"Hello, good sir Huxtable," Merritt said back with a smile, kneeling beside him to tuck his blankets around him. "Did you stay up reading?"

"Yeah, I wanted to finish it before bed but I got tired," he said, rubbing his eyes.

"I do that sometimes, too. It'll be there in the morning," Merritt offered, smoothing his red hair away from his forehead.

"Sure," Huxley said with a yawn, turning away from Merritt.

"Goodnight, bud," she said.

"Mer?" His little voice came in a whisper. "Will you rub my back to help me fall asleep again?"

She smiled in the dark. He needed her less and less these days, so it felt extra special when he did. "Of course." She sat on the edge of his bed and smoothed her palm over his back gently, lulling him back to sleep. It didn't take long until his breathing shifted to long, deep breaths, and she knew he'd passed out finally.

She sat there in the dark for a few moments longer to make sure he stayed asleep, basking in the quiet and dark. Maybe Dylan would be asleep by the time she got back. She stood and straightened a few toys out on the bookshelf, tossing his laundry into the hamper.

When she left his room, she ran into Rebekah standing in the entry to the laundry room, staring at the throw pillow case.

"Do I even want to know?" Rebekah asked, her gray hair pinned in a claw clip.

"Mashed potato mishap," Merritt said awkwardly.

Rebekah shook her head in disbelief.

"Why are you doing laundry so late?" Merritt asked. "Go get some rest."

"It's a neverending task, honey," Rebekah said. "Why don't *you* go get some rest?"

"My sleeping arrangements aren't exactly peaceful," Merritt said, crossing her arms.

Rebekah leveled her with the same impatient stare she gave her every time she complained about Dylan.

Merritt put her hands up in surrender and backed out of the room, retreating to the carriage house, praying that Dylan had gone to sleep early.

CHAPTER 4

Dylan was startled when Mrs. Vanlaningham popped her head into the kitchen but recovered without a full yelp of panic. Mrs. Vanlaningham didn't seem to notice. "We're having a few people over for dinner. Do you mind adding about four more?"

Dylan paused where she was standing over a piece of beef tenderloin that she was trussing. Sure, it was deeply inconvenient to be alerted at the last possible second that four more plates needed to be made, but what was she going to do, say no? Of course not. She was a professional, and she was going to make it work. Even if that meant spending the next couple of hours in a full panic. "Absolutely. Not a problem at all, Mrs. Vanlaningham."

Mrs. Vanlaningham smiled and rolled her eyes. "Oh, please. I've told you a dozen times, call me Julia."

Dylan nodded, knowing full well she'd probably never call her Julia to her face, given how formal Mr. Vanlaningham was. Had she ever seen the man without a tie? Did he wear one under his ski jacket?

As soon as Mrs. Vanlaningham—Julia—walked out of the room, Dylan washed her hands and opened up her notebook as she dried her fingers on the towel hooked over her apron waist. She scribbled a few notes about how to increase the size of the appetizers, what she could add into the side dishes to bulk them up a bit without losing flavor. A little voice in the back of her head said that she'd better find a more special dessert. She'd planned something simple, an apple pie brownie concoction with homemade ice cream, but a cake seemed like the better choice. Except she was terrible at cakes. She glanced at the clock over the oven, wondering if she had time to run down to the bakery in town. Maybe if she hurried. And sped a bit. And if there were no lines at any of the shops. And if parking wasn't a nightmare. She could also swing by the butcher and see if they had any more beef tenderloin while she was at it, which would justify the dessert change.

An hour later, she shuffled back in the kitchen, her arms full of packages of treats and meats. She'd lucked out and found a gorgeous decorated cake in the shape of a holiday wreath that would be the perfect centerpiece for dessert.

Merritt and Huxley walked into the kitchen, debating something that sounded an awful lot like whether Pluto should still technically be a planet. Honestly, it sounded like Merritt was losing, which tracked because Huxley was one of the most creepily precocious children that Dylan had ever met. She watched with trepidation as Huxley's eyes landed on the cellophane top of the cake box

"A cake? For me?" he asked.

Merritt snorted with amusement. "I don't think so, buddy, unless it's your birthday and you forgot to tell me, but I didn't take you for a Sagitarrius."

"It's my half birthday," he whined.

"It is not," Merritt said automatically, but Dylan could see her counting months in her head.

"It is!" He protested. "December 23 is my half birthday. Six months past June 23."

"Is it already December 23? Damn." Dylan said.

Huxley' eyes widened and his head snapped toward Merritt. "She said *damn.*"

Merritt put her hands on her hips and narrowed her eyes at Dylan, then glanced back to Huxley. "She can choose the words in her vocabulary differently because she's an adult. Most of the time."

Dylan feigned shock. "Most?" Merritt didn't answer but Dylan could have sworn she could see a small smile quirk the edge of her mouth.

"Can I have some of this cake then?" Huxley asked, eye on the prize.

"You'll have it with dinner, my man," Dylan said, sliding the cake away across the counter to help dissuade him. Or maybe just because her heart skipped a few beats thinking that something might happen to the perfect frosting.

Merritt seemed to sense her unease and ushered Huxley out of the kitchen in front of her. "Let's go read books in the window seat while it snows."

"You promised me hot chocolate first," Huxley said. "Plus, I don't need you to sit with me. You can go read somewhere else."

The kid sure had a sweet tooth and a lot of nerve.

Merritt sighed. "You're right about the hot chocolate, I guess, but don't think that I'm passing up an opportunity to read in the best seat in the house. You'll just have to share. You got me off track with the cake talk." Dylan watched Merritt walk to the pantry and pull down a Swiss Miss box. Dylan nearly gasped at the sight but stopped herself short of slapping it out of Merritt's hands.

"You're not seriously making hot chocolate from a packet when I'm here," Dylan said, grimacing.

Merritt glanced down to the box, then back up to Dylan. "Uh, yes?"

"I'll make you two hot chocolate."

Merritt glanced around at the mess of a kitchen. "Really? You seem... busy."

Truthfully, Dylan was in over her head with the meal. But she wasn't about to let them drink powdered hot chocolate when she was standing *right there*. And hot chocolate wasn't hard to make, necessarily. She could babysit the double broiler while toasting the bread for the stuffing.

"I'll bring it to you in a few," Dylan said, winking.

Merritt stared back at her blankly. "Okay."

"But I want hot chocolate now," Huxley whined as Merritt shooed him from the room.

"Don't worry, dude. It's gonna be worth the wait," Dylan said, suddenly wishing she had four extra arms.

Ten minutes later, she walked through the family room to the large window seat where Merritt and Huxley were tucked, toe to toe, noses stuck in thick books. Huxley was reading Narnia and the cover of Merritt's book suggested romance. Hmm, a romantic? She could work with that.

For a moment, Dylan longed to join them as they both took the mugs of hot chocolate with wide eyes.

"Careful, Hux. It could be hot," Merritt warned as Huxley nearly shoved his entire face into his mug, gulping.

"I made it a drinkable temperature so neither of you would have to wait," Dylan said with a smile.

Merritt looked up at her, an unreadable sentiment behind her dark eyes. Was that a tiny bit of warmth Dylan detected there? "Thanks," she said, sipping from the mug. Her eyes closed as she savored the flavor, making something stir low in Dylan's stomach.

"Better than Swiss Miss?"

Merritt nodded. "Barely. I miss the tiny marshmallows, but this will do."

Dylan grinned. "Sure." She headed back to the kitchen, smiling to herself in a cheesy way that made her feel like a preteen with a crush. That smile faded the moment she realized she was burning the bread, though. She rushed to the oven and grabbed a towel to wave off the smoke as she snatched the pan out.

Two hours later, dinner was about to be served, and she'd managed to salvage what would pass as a delicious homemade meal from a classically-trained chef. She brushed off her hands and wiped her hair away from her face, walking with Rebekah into the dining room to introduce the first course. Mr. and Mrs. Vanlaningham were seated at opposite ends of a large table, with four others on either side of the table. She wondered briefly where Huxley was, but guessed he'd eaten with Merritt early. She couldn't blame the kid or the parents for not wanting an eight-year-old attending a grown up dinner party. She explained the course and meal overall as she leaned over and topped off Mr. Vanlaningham's wine glass, trying her best to be cordial and approachable in case anyone had questions. One of her biggest pet peeves was inaccessible food—if she had to google what a menu item or preparation meant, she was frustrated, so she couldn't imagine what it was like for those who hadn't gone to culinary school.

She returned to the kitchen, making the final preparations on the main course of the meal, pouring the sauce she'd prepared into the gravy boat. But something wasn't... right. She couldn't put her finger on exactly where the feeling was coming from, but she'd worked long enough in professional and private kitchens to listen to that little voice in her head that made her unnerved. As she looked around, she couldn't help but think she'd forgotten something, or maybe something had been messed with. That was when she saw it. The cake box was just slightly askew on the counter, one edge torn as if it was hastily opened and closed.

Dread pooled in her stomach and she reached for the box in slow-motion, the cardboard squeaked against the counter as she slid it towards her. Maybe she was just being overly cautious. Maybe she was being paranoid. She really hoped she was being cautiously paranoid.

She flipped open the lid and cursed. The frosting was smeared over the top of the cake with what seemed to be the exact size of an eight-year-old's hand. Though the hard evidence was lacking, only one member of the family had been excited enough about the cake to reach an entire hand in and scoop up almost every topping.

"What's wrong?" Merritt asked, standing across the island with a cup of tea in her hands. "You look like the Grinch stole all your presents."

"Worse," Dylan croaked.

Although Merritt's expression wasn't exactly empathetic, she did look curious and confused. Maybe Dylan should chalk it up to a win that her expression wasn't outright glee-ful. "What happened?"

"*Someone*, and I'm not naming names, but *someone* swiped all of the frosting off of the top of this goddamn cake," Dylan said, her jaw clenched tight.

Merritt's eyes widened and she leaned forward as Dylan dropped the entire lid of the cake box open to reveal the mangled confection. She paused, slowly sipping her tea. "I suppose you have a culprit in mind?"

Dylan's eyes widened. Normally she'd love to stand there and banter with Merritt all day long, but this was a crisis. Could she salvage it? Could she still make the apple pie brownie bars? She barely recognized the fact that Merritt had set down her mug and was opening the pantry, standing right in the way of where Dylan needed to start grabbing ingredi-ents. Even though Merritt was nearly five or six inches shorter than her and she could *technically* reach above and around the woman, she was still terribly in the way.

"What could you *possibly need* at this moment?" Dylan snapped, impatience making her tone sharp as a knife's edge.

Merritt said nothing, but Dylan watched as she reached for the powdered sugar, then made her way to the fridge for milk and butter, piling everything into her arms to set on the kitchen island.

"What are you doing?" Dylan asked, still impatient but slightly more curious.

"Making buttercream," Merritt said casually, as though she was simply picking out a sweater for the day. She washed her hands in the sink and dried them on a clean towel.

Dylan tilted her head. "How do you know how to make buttercream?"

"I worked in a bakery in college," Merritt said, measuring out ingredients.

Dylan wanted to ask if Merritt actually had any skill when it came to icing—after all, she was terrible at it, so she didn't have much faith in a non-chef's abilities. But, this seemed like a favor, and Merritt wasn't prone to random acts of kindness towards her right now, so she stayed silent.

"How much time do we have?" Merritt asked, grabbing the stand mixer from the opposite counter. She moved with purpose, like she was used to being in the kitchen, used to commanding a meal. Dylan idly wondered if she cooked for Huxley back in New York.

"Forty-five minutes?" Dylan squeaked, wanting to throw up at the realization. "If I pour the wine liberally."

"Plenty of time," Merritt said, looking in the drawers under the kitchen island. "Any palette knives or bench scrapers around?"

"Uh, afraid not. I'm not much of a baker," Dylan confessed.

Merritt grabbed out a butter knife and two spoons. Dylan cringed. Oh god, this was going downhill fast.

Dylan raked a hand through the hair that had begun slipping out of her bun. "I could probably whip something up so you don't have to bother. Or I could make... uh, cake pops or something." Cake pops? Could she really picture serving cake pops to the Vanlaninghams? Well, maybe Huxley, but definitely not anyone else.

Merritt turned and placed a hand on Dylan's shoulder. "I need you to take a deep breath."

Dylan did as she was told. She stared down at Merritt, those dark chocolate eyes staring back up at her. Flashes of last Christmas came to her then, not only the nights tangled in sheets, but the days of grins and stolen kisses and spending a day off walking around town hand in hand. Tenderness clenched in her chest.

"And I need you to shut the fuck up," Merritt said in the same commanding tone.

Okay, a *little* bit of the tenderness dissipated.

"I'm going to fix this cake, and you're going to just trust me, because what other choice do you have?" Merritt nodded once, staring up at her with determination on her face, then after she apparently decided Dylan wasn't going to get in her way or question her any more, she turned back to the cake. "You might want to carve up your meat," Merritt added, a stray strand of dark hair falling across her forehead.

Oh, fuck. The rest of the meal was on the counter, ready to be plated. How long had it been since she served the first course? That damn cake had her so out of sorts. And Merritt's presence on top of that... Dylan took a deep breath and got to work.

When she returned from serving the main course, she found Merritt painstakingly painting the cake with a green buttercream, creating each leaf of the wreath with a butter knife and spoon on a piece of parchment paper, then placing the leaf on the cake. It looked... really good. Professional, even. She'd scraped all of the mangled buttercream off the cake and smoothed it to perfection. Dylan watched Merritt's delicate fingers move deftly as she put finishing touches on her masterpiece.

"Whoa, where'd you learn to do that?" Dylan asked.

"Don't sound so surprised that I'm good at something," Merritt growled.

"No, that's not what I meant. I'm just saying, that doesn't look like a hobby," Dylan said, wiping her forehead with the back of her hand.

"I told you, I worked in a bakery in college," Merritt said, her olive-toned cheeks flushing.

"Like, a really impressive bakery, apparently," Dylan added.

Merritt snorted but didn't look up from the tiny holly berries she was now dotting the wreath with. One might never guess a child had dunked their hand in it mere moments before.

Speaking of... "Where's Huxley?" Dylan asked.

"He's in bed, reading," Merritt said, her tongue sticking out in concentration. It was truly adorable. "He kicked me out once I started questioning him about why his hand and mouth were green."

"Caught green handed." Dylan smirked. She eyed the way Merritt piped a ribbon using a ziplock bag onto the wreath, smoothing it with the butter knife.

"He's a good kid, but he doesn't need me to watch him like a hawk like he used to. Now he just lacks impulse control around cake. Which, you know, I can't blame him," Merritt said, stepping back from the counter to inspect the cake. "Okay, it's not my best work, but it's good enough."

Dylan looked down at the finished cake. "Are you kidding me? This looks gorgeous."

Merritt's mouth quirked up in a smile. "I know, right?"

Before Dylan could second-guess herself, she stepped forward and pulled Merritt into a hug. "Thank you for your help."

Merritt was stiff against her, but for a moment, Dylan felt her relax into the embrace. god, it felt good to hold her again. She'd forgotten how well they fit together, Merritt's head tucking neatly into the crook of her shoulder and neck. Merritt patted her shoulder. "No problem," she said, taking a step back. Dylan immediately felt the loss of her, wanting nothing more than to pull her back again.

Merritt cleared her throat and wiped her hands on a towel, hurrying out of the kitchen with some excuse about checking on Huxley. Dylan watched her leave, feeling like she should have never let Merritt go without the promise of more last year.

CHAPTER 5

MERRITT

Merritt stared down at her Kindle, not registering a single word she was reading. Her mind reeled from being back in Dylan's arms again. She tightened the covers around her—though she'd been tucked in bed for nearly a half hour, Dylan hadn't made it back to the carriage house yet. She was somehow both dreading and looking forward to the moment that Dylan stepped through that door. Just one innocent hug and she'd gone and felt all of the things again. Dylan's warm scent, like spiced cider, and the way she always hugged tightly, like she never wanted to let go. Like Merritt was something precious.

She rubbed her eyes. god, she was reading too many romances. She closed the cover of her Kindle and pulled out her phone. This was the kind of crisis that required the group chat.

Merritt typed out a message about how Dylan had hugged her.

"Seems innocent enough," Kylie wrote back almost immediately. Typical. Kylie was always rational.

"Noooooo," Ezra wrote. "Don't fall for that!"

"Fall for what?" she asked.

"The classic Dylan seduction!" Ezra wrote.

"A little dramatic, Ez." That was Kylie. "Merritt helped her, and she was grateful. Doesn't mean she is ready to settle down."

Ezra wrote back almost immediately. "No more Christmas flings. I cannot stand hearing about this woman again all year."

Her poor friends had a point. They'd spent the entire year hearing about Dylan—well, they'd heard plenty the first few months of the year, and then Merritt had managed to taper it down to only random bouts of melancholy when she'd had a little too much wine.

A FaceTime call popped up from the group and Merritt reached for her headphones, hitting Join as she put the pods in her ears.

When their two screens popped up, Kylie was lying in bed in near darkness, but Ezra was sitting on the couch with gold undereye masks on.

"Why don't you just ask her what's going on?" Kylie said.

"What am I supposed to say?" Merritt asked.

Ezra rolled their eyes. "You could start with, 'Why the fuck didn't you text me back for a year?'"

"A little blunt," Kylie said with a laugh.

"Merritt's a little blunt," Ezra said, to which Kylie nodded.

"I am not," Merritt said, shaking her head.

"Yeah, you're right, you're being extremely passive-aggressive here," Ezra said, taking a bite of what looked like an Oreo.

"Ez, tell me you're not just sitting on the couch eating cookies and watching Sister Wives," Kylie said.

"You bet your sweet ass I am," they said with a wink.

"I wish I had cookies." Merritt's stomach grumbled. She'd had a few crackers for dinner, but had gotten distracted by

Huxley and the cake when she'd gone to find more food, also known as stealing some of the leftovers from dinner. Dylan was a damn good cook, that much was true. Not that she'd ever admit that to Dylan, but she looked forward to grabbing bites of everything that woman made.

"Want me to talk to the chef at your hotel?" Ezra said with a mouthful of Oreo.

Kylie groaned. "I've got a client meeting tomorrow, can I go to bed now?"

"It's only 11:30 pm in New York, you big baby," Merritt said with a grin.

"What's the case this time?" Ezra asked.

"That's confidential," Kylie said, haughtily shaking her head.

"Sex scandal," both Merritt and Ezra said in monotone tandem, then giggled like they were the funniest two people in the world. Kylie's law firm handled some big name cases, but usually when she was being a little too secretive, it was because some man had been an asshole.

Kylie rolled her eyes. "Goodnight, you dweebs."

"Goodnight," Merritt sing-songed, waving as she clicked the off button. She glanced up as the front door of the carriage house opened and she heard Dylan kick off her shoes. Her stomach flipped, nervous flutters attacking her insides. Why was she so nervous to see Dylan?

She hurriedly grabbed her Kindle and flipped it open, trying to appear as though she had been reading instead of gossiping with her friends. But why should she care what Dylan thought? Talking shit with her friends was one of her favorite hobbies.

And it wasn't like they were only talking about Dylan, after all. They talked about cookies and sex scandals to really round out the topics. Kylie's advice swirled in her head about simply asking Dylan what had happened, but she was too embarrassed to broach the topic. And maybe too sober. But mostly she didn't want to seem desperate or needy. Nothing seemed worse than being desperate for a woman like Dylan, who knew exactly how irresistible she was. Gorgeous, sexy, perfect hands, that disarming smile... not to mention all of her other talents. Dylan was the kind of girl *everyone* was thirsty for, and that had to be tiring eventually, right?

"Are you hungry?" Dylan called out from the kitchenette area. Merritt could hear her opening a cupboard and knocking around dishes.

Out of curiosity and *not* desperation, Merritt climbed out of bed and walked down the hall to the living area to find Dylan plating a quesadilla, her hair pulled into a high bun and her sleeves rolled up to the elbow, showing off her colorful tattoos. "Hey," Merritt said, nodding toward the plate. "What's this?"

Dylan glanced up at Merritt through her lashes. "I thought you might not have eaten dinner, so I made you a quesadilla, just in case."

"You made me a just-in-case-adilla?" Merritt asked with a smirk.

Dylan's green eyes crinkled with an incredulous look as she burst out laughing. "Yeah, a just-in-case-adilla."

"I am a little hungry," Merritt said, not reaching for the plate as she sat down on one of the barstools at the small island that doubled as a table. Dylan slid the just-in-case-adilla across the counter toward her, then grabbed sour cream and salsa out of the small fridge. "How did you know I didn't eat?" she asked, dipping a slice of the quesadilla into a dollop of sour cream.

"I didn't see you eat and you didn't ask me for anything," Dylan said with a shrug, pulling a beer out of the fridge. She held one up as if to offer it to Merritt, who nodded and reached out to take the can.

"How do you know I didn't make something myself? You're not *my* personal chef." Merritt cracked the tab of the beer open as she resisted the groan of delicious approval after taking a bite of the quesadilla, holding a hand over her mouth to chew the large bite she'd taken. She never realized how hungry she was until she was eating, which was a terrible survival instinct.

"Yeah, but I like cooking for you," Dylan said, grinning crookedly as she sipped her beer, her one dimple taunting Merritt yet again.

"Don't do that," Merritt said, pointing a sharp finger at her as she drank from her own beer.

"Do what?" Dylan said, leaning a hip onto the counter.

Merritt gestured broadly. "That."

"This?" Dylan said, continuing to smile as flames danced between them in the heat of her stare.

"Yes," said Merritt, exasperated. She turned in her seat, holding her quesadilla plate as she looked away from Dylan, who she could hear chuckling.

"Okay, okay, I'll tone it down," Dylan said, clearing her throat. She pulled out her phone and softened at the screen in a way that made Merritt feel just a tiny bit jealous. Who was on the receiving end of that look?

Merritt peaked over her shoulder, blinded by the dimple in Dylan's cheek as she smiled. "That's not toned down," she accused, but couldn't help but laugh at the absurdity of the request. She was scared of how much she enjoyed being around Dylan again. She couldn't get sucked back into what she thought they had last year.

"Hey," Dylan said, her voice low as she slipped her phone back into her pocket. "Is the quesadilla not tasting right? I can remake it."

Merritt hadn't realized she'd let her thoughts show on her face. "No, the food is good."

Dylan didn't say more, but watched her as she took another drink from her beer. "Alright, out with it."

"Out with what?" Merritt asked, dread creeping into her

chest. She did not want to get into this right now. Not when they had to spend the next week and a half together.

"You obviously have something on your mind." Dylan set down her beer can and placed her hands on the counter.

Kylie's advice sounded less and less like a good idea with each passing moment of Dylan's intense stare. Merritt gulped. "What do you expect me to say?"

"I don't know, but I'd love for you to start with why you're treating me like I killed your childhood parakeet."

"I didn't have a parakeet." Wow, that kind of deflection and tangent was almost too easy. Maybe she could just not discuss her feelings and talk about her childhood guinea pigs, Debra and Donna. Debbie and Donnie had plenty of tales she could talk up that would definitely not include her having to tell Dylan that she—

"Merritt, come on. You know what I mean."

Merritt stared down longingly at the quesadilla she hadn't finished yet. Well, now she wouldn't be able to, knowing it was a bribe in order to get her to talk about her feelings. "It's nothing." A last ditch effort but not a terrible one.

Dylan didn't say anything, but continued to stare her down all the same.

She gulped, tugging at the mock neck of her sweater. Was it hot in here? Was her collar too tight? Was she about to suffocate to death? Maybe all of the above, if she was lucky.

"I thought we had a really good time last year," Dylan began, her tone quiet and soft like a hand reaching out for another in the dark.

"I thought so, too," Merritt confessed.

"So, then why are you acting like this?" Dylan said, clearly exasperated but keeping it together quite well.

"Childhood parakeets aside—"

"Mer."

"You never called me," Merritt said finally, holding up her hands. "Is that what you want to hear? That I was really sad

that it was just a fling for you and I thought it was more? That
I was mad that I never heard from you again?"

Dylan stared at her, her mouth hanging a tiny bit slack
with shock.

"We had a great time last year, and maybe I was naive but
I really thought it wasn't going to end there."

"I thought you *wanted* it to," Dylan said, her brow creasing
in the middle.

"What? Why would I have wanted it to?" Merritt asked,
feeling like she had missed a vital part of a past conversation.

Dylan ran both hands through her hair, holding them on
top of her head as she blew out a deep breath. The movement
made her shirt pull up slightly, revealing the Calvin Klein
branding on the band of her underwear,peeking over the
edge of her jeans. Dear god, could the woman be *any* more
distracting?

"You kept making these comments about it only being for
a few weeks, and your life back in New York, and how the
Vanlaninghams only made the trip to Snowy Springs at
Christmas, so you had no reason to come back to Colorado,
and... I just... I thought you were politely telling me where we
stood."

"You were just fine with it being a holiday fling?" Merritt
asked, crossing her arms.

"I think you're missing my point on purpose," Dylan said,
her eyebrows raising patiently as though she was willing to
wait for Merritt to sift back through the supplied information
to find the real point.

Shame and embarrassment burned Merritt's cheeks and
she held her palms to her face. "I thought that was what you
wanted to hear," she mumbled into her hands.

Dylan let her hands fall back to her sides. "In what world
would I want to hear that you didn't want this to progress
further? Why did you never text *me*?"

"I did text you. Almost right away. And then never again

because I didn't want to be the desperate clinger you're probably used to," Merritt said, her hands still over her face.

Dylan didn't say anything for another moment, and Merritt wondered if she was silently agreeing. Instead, she heard Dylan's feet on the floor as it creaked beneath her, and then Dylan's hands were on her own, pulling them from hiding her face. She was leaning down, eye to eye with Merritt. "You are absurd."

"Hey," Merritt said, pushing Dylan's shoulder lightly.

Dylan laughed. "I mean it. You built up so much resentment over, what, some playgirl version of me you'd made up in your head?"

Merritt slumped her shoulders. "When you say it like that..." She looked down to the place where Dylan's hands still held hers, warm and strong and soft all at once.

"If I ever made you feel like you were just some fling, I apologize. That was my mistake," Dylan said, and Merritt wanted to crawl inside a kitchen cabinet to die of embarrassment. Instead, she just nodded. "Let's just forget last year."

Merritt snapped her face up to look at Dylan. "What?"

"Let's forget it and start over."

Merritt raised a skeptical eyebrow. "Start over?"

Dylan let go of Merritt's hands, then held one of hers out. "Hey, I'm Dylan. I'm a chef."

Merritt pressed her mouth into a thin line. "We're really doing this?"

Dylan's eyes crinkled at the edges. "Play along or I'll never make you another quesadilla ever again."

Merritt sighed, trying to hide her smile, as she reached and shook Dylan's hand. "Nice to meet you. I'm Merritt. I'm a nanny."

Dylan nodded. "Well, Merritt. It's nice to meet you. I hope I'll see you around." She winked, then stood, and walked into the bedroom.

※

LATER THAT NIGHT, Merritt watched Dylan in the dim light coming in through the window. Dylan slept so fitfully, kicking covers and battling her pillow. She didn't remember that from last year.

Could they really start over? Had it really just been a stupid miscommunication that kept them from talking for an entire year? It was one thing to move from a misunderstanding to common ground, but an entirely other issue to transition from utmost resentment and a healthy dose of embarrassment to finding their footing again.

Could they? And, more importantly, did she want to?

After all, in a week, she'd be back in New York, and Dylan would still be in Colorado, basically a world away.

As she studied Dylan's slightly crooked nose and the way her lips parted as she exhaled, Merritt couldn't help but wonder what else she didn't remember from last year, and what she hadn't known in the first place. A flock of nervous butterflies swirled in her stomach at the thought that Dylan would have to get to know her again, too. Would she like what she found?

CHAPTER 6

Dylan stretched in bed. It was Christmas Eve, and more importantly, it was her day off. The Vanlaninghams were at a family gathering, so she was free to do as she pleased. She had a big day tomorrow, so she had made zero plans for today in order to rest up and recover from a long week, not to mention prep to make sure Christmas dinner was a success.

She glanced sideways toward the window to see what time of morning it was, and not just to check if Merritt was still around. She smiled immediately upon seeing that Merritt was still asleep—well, that and the morning light still looked faint.

Merritt looked peaceful while she slept, so unlike when she was awake. It was fascinating to see her face completely without expression—no glares, no smirks, no eye rolling. She was as still as a statue. An intrusive thought about checking if Merritt was breathing crept into her brain, and she sat up in a panic, leaning toward Merritt's bed.

"What? What's wrong?" Merritt said, her eyes suddenly

open.

"Damn, you're a light sleeper," Dylan said, shaking her head.

"It comes with the job. That kid just *appears* sometimes," Merritt said, rubbing her eyes and picking up her phone to check the time. "It's 7 am. Go back to bed or go get me coffee."

"You don't have to go hang out with Huxley?" Dylan asked, stretching again as she stood. She noticed Merritt's eyes take in the skin that bared between her shirt and shorts, then glance away quickly with a bit of color to her cheeks. Dylan stretched again, hands higher over her head, because she *had* to, and not because she just wanted to give Merritt a bit more to see. Being a chef was physical work, and she was sore. Absolutely no devious plan here.

"They're at Kellen's parents. And Julia gave me the day off tomorrow, too," Merritt said, grabbing her phone.

"Two days in a row? You lucky duck."

"I know, it's a Christmas miracle. I guess Julia wants to hang out with her kid on a major holiday? Weird," Merritt joked. "I'm serious about that coffee, though." She brushed some of her bedhead curls out of her face as she began looking at her phone screen.

"Let's go get some," Dylan offered.

Merritt grimaced. "It's cold and early and I don't want to shower yet."

Dylan threw a beanie her way. "So, wear this."

Merritt groaned. "Oh my god, how in the world do you wake up so chipper and ready to go? It's really disconcerting."

"Disconcerting?" Dylan asked, grabbing a sweatshirt and pulling sweatpants on over her sleep shorts.

"Yeah, like now I'm wondering if maybe you're a serial killer," Merritt said, sitting up and wrapping herself in her blankets. "Next you're going to tell me you don't use a phone case."

Dylan paused. "Um, I don't."

Merritt stared at her, blinking slowly. "Absolutely sociopathic."

Dylan snorted, amused. "Come on, I'll drive."

Dylan watched Merritt tugging on the edge of the beanie, trying to get it to lie properly over her curls. "You look nice. Stop fidgeting," she said, one hand on the small of Merritt's back as they paused to open the door to the Blizzard Cafe.

The inside of the cafe was decorated floor to ceiling in Christmas decor—trees, garlands, lights, a mural of reindeer flying through the sky, an entire army of wintery gnomes lining the confections display case. The barista was dressed as Mrs. Claus and every drink was named for a Christmas or holiday theme. Really, this town really loved Christmas.

"Tell me you have some impossibly complicated coffee order," Dylan teased as they stood in line.

"And if I did? What's it to you?" Merritt said, raising her eyebrows. "Making fun of things that women like that hurt literally no one—"

Dylan raised her hands in surrender. "I was just going to say that it couldn't possibly be more complicated than mine."

Merritt paused, looking puzzled. The expression made Dylan laugh as they stepped up to order at the counter. Merritt ordered a drip coffee with cream, which was such a boring order, and Dylan ordered a Peppermint Kisses latte, with only half of the usual pumps of peppermint syrup, extra mocha, oatmilk, and extra whip. Merritt eyed her but didn't say a word, though it was clear by her smile that she found Dylan's drink amusing. Sure, it was something a thirteen-year-old might order, but she liked what she liked.

"To stay or to go?" The barista asked.

"To go—" Merritt started.

"To stay, please," Dylan interrupted as she held up her card to pay.

"Another case of food bribery, I see," Merritt said, rolling her eyes, but Dylan could see by the tug of a grin at the corner of her mouth that she wasn't actually annoyed. Merritt was only hard to read if one didn't know the language, and Dylan was fascinated to translate more and more as she learned.

They found a seat near the window, which was painted with white snowflakes of course, and waited for their drinks to be called. Silence settled between them as they both looked around. Dylan wondered if Merritt was also wondering if this counted as a first date. The air was slightly awkward and tense between them, and it occurred to Dylan then that they'd spent so little time *talking* last year. Who were they outside of their jobs? To help ease the mood, Dylan cleared her throat and folded her hands on the table, straightening. "So, Merritt Perkins, where do you see yourself in five years?"

Merritt laughed softly. "Well, Huxley will be 13, so—"

"Not where Huxley will be in five years. You."

Merritt shrugged. "Maybe still being just a nanny, I guess."

"*Just* the nanny?" Dylan raised an eyebrow.

"Yes?" Merritt answered, confused.

"I don't know, it seems like a fucking hard job. I don't think I'd downplay it if I were you," Dylan answered.

"It isn't easy, and I love Huxley, but it's not like my *dream* job," Merritt admitted.

"What's your dream job?" Dylan asked, interrupted by the barista calling out her name with their drinks. She stood quickly and got the drinks, walking carefully back to the table.

"That's a personal question for someone I've only just met last night," Merritt teased, her voice dipping lower, swirling in velvety sweetness. Oh dear god, that was a dangerous combination.

"Indulge me," Dylan said, sipping her latte and trying not to think of what Merritt's tone brought to mind. It was a burst of sweetness and mint and chocolate, blending together perfectly. She closed her eyes in bliss, licking the extra whipped cream off her mouth before going in for another sip. When she glanced toward a very quiet Merritt, she saw the woman looking at her with the kind of intensity Dylan usually reserved for memorizing new recipes.

Dylan wiped at her mouth with a napkin. "If you want, I'll go first. My dream job is to move to a big city with a lot of culture so I can learn more and maybe improve and find my own style, then write a book, that kind of thing."

"Aren't you already a private chef full time? What more is there to learn?" Merritt asked, tilting her head.

Dylan shook her head. "I mean, I've got a bunch of clients, but everyone is only a few meals a week. It's fine, it's not hard, and it's good money, and it's been great for my restless style, but I just... want something *more* for myself for the first time in a long time. I don't know, it's kind of silly, I guess." She'd never admitted that to anyone. She'd always prided herself on being a rolling stone and her ability to make her own schedule, so it seemed ridiculous to want more structure and more training. But she had felt stagnantin her career and wanted to keep moving forward, not just stay in place. Maybe her restlessness about the rest of her life had just transferred over to her professional life. She took another drink, twisting the realization around in her head.

"It's not silly to want something more," Merritt said. "Is this a new dream? I feel like we never talked about this last year."

"We didn't do much talking last year," Dylan said with a wink.

Merritt balked, her eyes wide as she looked around the crowded cafe. "Dylan," she scolded, scandalized.

Dylan laughed. "I'd forgotten what a prude you are."

Merritt leveled her with a look, lowering her voice. "I think you probably remember very well how much I am, in fact, the very opposite of a prude."

Dylan looked up with a smile, and couldn't help but reminisce fondly. "Ah, yes, I remember."

Merritt blushed and let out a huff of a laugh in a way that made Dylan's chest clench. "Okay, so you want to move to a big city and learn more. What's that entail? Like, getting a mentor or working at a world-class restaurant?" Merritt asked.

Dylan shrugged. "Something like that."

"Come on, indulge me." Merritt sipped her own coffee, holding the mug in both of her hands. Her nails were perfectly manicured and painted a deep, rich burgundy color. It was wrong for Dylan to picture those fingers along her own bare skin, right?

She cleared her throat again, realizing she was clenching her cup in both fists, knuckles almost white. "I think you're deflecting away from your dream job."

"I don't have one," Merritt admitted. "I don't *dream* of having a job."

"Ah, so you're just waiting for a sugar mama," Dylan teased.

Merritt laughed, shaking her head. "No, not at all. I mean, I'm not saying that wouldn't be nice. I'd be a stay-at-home dog mom in a heartbeat."

Dylan grew excited at the premise. "You have a dog?"

"No, but like every childless person our age, I want one."

"A fair point."

"Okay, I really want to go back for my PhD," Merritt said with the kind of haste that made Dylan wonder if she'd ever said the words out loud before. "And then figure it out from there."

Dylan's eyebrows raised and she reached across the table to squeeze Merritt's hand. "That's awesome. What do you want to get your PhD in?"

"Child psychology," Merritt said, pressing her lips together.

"That's so interesting," Dylan said, leaning forward. "Huh. You must really like kids."

Merritt snorted. "Not all kids."

"What would you research?"

Merritt paused as though she was considering what to say, then sighed and said, "I'm fascinated by emotional development in early childhood."

Dylan's eyebrows raised in surprise. "I've never thought of that."

Merritt nodded slowly.

"What made you want to research that?" Dylan asked.

"Have I ever told you I'm the oldest of six?" Merritt asked.

Dylan shook her head.

"My very youngest sibling is fourteen years younger than I am," Merritt continued. "So I've just always been around kids. Helping to raise them, watching over them. It's what made Julia ask me to babysit Huxley originally."

"I always wondered how you got in with the Vanlaninghams."

"Yeah, Julia was one of my grad school professors, actually. She taught my favorite child psychology courses and she advised my Masters thesis."

"Also on kid feelings?" Dylan asked, desperate to keep Merritt talking, sharing about herself.

"Actually, it was research about how having older children be caretakers of younger siblings can really fuck them up developmentally," Merritt said with a laugh.

Dylan started with surprise. "Oh?" What else was she going to say? She waited, leaving the space for Merritt to continue if she wanted.

"I'm way less bitter about it now," Merritt said, waving a hand dismissively. "What about you? What's your family like?"

"I don't talk to them," Dylan said slowly, looking down into her drink.

"I don't talk to my parents either," Merritt said cheerfully, reaching up a hand for a high-five.

Dylan couldn't help but laugh, high-fiving Merritt back. "Makes the holidays kind of weird, though," she admitted.

Merritt watched her, nodding. "Makes working over the holidays nice, don't you think?"

Dylan nodded. "Exactly."

"How long have you been estranged from your family?" Merritt asked. "If you don't mind me asking."

Dylan shrugged. "I don't mind you asking me anything."

Merritt smiled softly.

"I was eighteen, so... sixteen years. A long time."

Merritt nodded. "It is."

Dylan couldn't put her finger on why she wanted to be so open with Merritt, especially about her family, who she never talked about. There was something in the way Merritt watched her that made her feel seen, like maybe no one had ever had the patience to hold time and space for Dylan to work out her thoughts and feelings. "They weren't religious or anything. Just total narcissists."

"I'm sorry to hear that," Merritt said softly. "That sounds really hard to deal with as a kid."

Something about that sounded familiar. The air was too tense between them, and Dylan felt too vulnerable. She could feel Merritt tapping at her walls—the same way she was trying to tap on Merritt's emotional walls, truthfully—and didn't love the idea of letting her guard down just yet. She wanted to be carefree, fun Dylan, not melancholy, family-problems Dylan. And she had the power to choose. "Oh my god, are you therapizing me right now?" Dylan asked, half-laughing with surprise. "Psychology major, I should have known."

Merritt's eyes widened in what seemed like dismay. "I didn't mean to make you feel like that," she said quickly, shaking her head. "I am only asking as a friend."

Dylan shrugged and smiled again, trying to lighten the mood. Was she teasing? Was she simply neutralizing the tension? Who was to say? "What's keeping you from going for the PhD?"

"Julia," Merritt groaned.

"What? Why?"

"Well, she's my employer, right? But she's also someone I need for a reference letter. And she's friends with the person who runs the Infant and Child Development lab at NYU Steinhardt, so I need her for that in, too."

"I'm not following how this is a bad situation for you."

Merritt chewed her lower lip. "How do I ask my employer to help me quit my job?"

Dylan nodded. "Ah, I see."

"I love the Vanlaninghams like they're family. They're really the only family I have. Do I give that up now? When Huxley is finally doing well in school and Julia isn't losing hair from stress and Kellen is still recovering from having a heart attack a year ago?" Merritt asked, looking more miserable with each question.

Dylan reached across the table, taking Merritt's hand in hers. "Correct me if I'm wrong, but didn't you just tell me you studied the effects of being the oldest child raising your younger siblings?"

Merritt raised an eyebrow. "Yeah?"

Dylan waited, wondering if it was her place to continue. Was she overstepping? Was she making assumptions? "You worry a lot about other people's feelings, but not your own."

Merritt shrugged, finishing her coffee. "What's next on the agenda?"

Dylan grinned. "You really want to keep hanging out?"

"I am caffeinated and at your disposal."

"Wow, you sure know how to make a girl feel special." Dylan stood from the table.

Merritt snorted, following suit. "Lead the way."

CHAPTER 7

Although Merritt hadn't had "grocery shop and cook a meal together" on her Christmas Eve bingo card, she didn't mind the current scene—the two of them side-by-side in the kitchen, the last light of the day fading in the windows. It always felt later than it was around the Winter Solstice, when the sun set at damn near 4:30 pm.

Dylan had been talking about Christmas dinner like it was her Superbowl and she was determined to win. If one could win Christmas dinner. Still, she didn't put it past Dylan to be the first winner of a holiday meal in world history.

Despite it being both of their days off, she stood at the counter washing and peeling carrots, a job she'd been suckered into because the alternative was preparing the elaborate sculpture of pork crown roast and she wasn't going anywhere near that. Dylan had several sheets of paper on the bench with what preparations to make the night before, given the elaborate nature of tomorrow's meal. The Vanlaninghams extended family would be joining, and Dylan had the exciting task of pleasing a group of of the most opinionated people she'd ever met.

Kacey Musgraves crooned about a present without a bow on a speaker sitting on the counter and Dylan hummed along, lost in her own little world. Merritt couldn't help but steal a few glances her way—after all, a look couldn't hurt, right? Dylan swayed to the music, her strong hands cutting away meat from the bones, then wrapped it around a cylinder to make the crown shape. Her sweater was rolled to the elbow, and her decorated forearms flexed with the effort. She worked methodically, and Merritt could tell that she loved what she did, even down to the most tedious tasks.

"Where'd you learn to do that?" Merritt asked. "It looks so fussy."

"Where all great chefs learn all of their secrets," Dylan said matter-of-factly, stabbing the pork with a skewer to help it hold its shape as she tied the twine.

Merritt raised an eyebrow. "Culinary school?"

"Watching Ina Garten make food for Jeffrey on Barefoot Contessa," Dylan said with a sly smile.

Merritt laughed in surprise.

"After all, food is the best expression of love, don't you think?" Dylan said, looking up and winking at her. Those green eyes twinkled with good humor.

Merritt looked at her skeptically. "I suppose so," she said. She thought back to their conversation in the coffee shop— was this entire year truly just a misunderstanding? An entire year spent resenting Dylan for no palpable reason?

They finished their tasks in silence, Dylan still humming and swaying to Christmas music, and Merritt trying not to think that it was comfortable to be doing something like cooking together. If Dylan hadn't ghosted her, would they have spent more nights cooking together in the kitchen just like this? Well, maybe a smaller kitchen, since this one was definitely not in her personal budget, with two wall ovens, a massive kitchen island bigger than her first apartment, and a countertop stone she was pretty sure cost more than her entire education.

"Pie time," Dylan said, clapping her hands together.

"What kind of pie are you making?" Merritt asked, wiping her hands on a towel.

"Pumpkin, obviously. And a chocolate bourbon tart," Dylan said, reaching for her printed recipe papers.

"A chocolate bourbon tart? That sounds right up Kellen's alley," Merritt said. "Those are his two favorite things."

"Exactly," Dylan said, tapping her temple. "Not just a pretty face."

"Oh, please," Merritt said, rolling her eyes.

Dylan grabbed pastry she'd refrigerated the day before, and began assembling the crust as she put Merritt on the finicky task of melting sugar into bourbon in a saucepan on the stove. Dylan poured two extra glasses of bourbon, offering one to Merritt to sip as she stirred the mixture. The chef appeared over her shoulder, watching her work.

"I'm not gonna burn it," Merritt said, feeling a little offended that Dylan was watching her so closely.

"I didn't say you were," Dylan said, her breath warm on Merritt's cheek. That woman was entirely too close, her spiced scent clouding Merritt's judgement. If Merritt took too deep of a breath in, her entire body would brush against Dylan's. She stilled as Dylan reached past her and dipped a finger in the bourbon sauce, bringing it to her mouth.

The entire world tipped slightly as she watched Dylan's tongue trail over her fingertip. Such an innocent gesture and dear god, such a sexy one at the same time. "How's it taste?" she croaked, desperate to break the tension from Dylan's close presence and taste-test.

"Here, try it for yourself," Dylan said, her voice lowering as her finger skimmed the surface of the liquid, then brushed against Merritt's lip. Merritt's tongue flicked out before she could think better of it, her eyes lifting to Dylan's as she moved to take Dylan's finger in her mouth, the richness and sweetness of the liquid sparking on her tongue. The movement was slow and lingering. Dylan's eyelids lowered as she watched Merritt, and before Merritt could even comprehend what was happening, Dylan's finger was replaced by her mouth.

The sweet taste of Dylan's lips on hers made her forget every worry, every resentment, and her arms wrapped around Dylan's shoulders instinctively. Oh, how goddamn good it felt to have Dylan back in her arms, kissing her again. Dylan's mouth was steady against hers—not desperate and sloppy, but assured. Dylan was taking her time, claiming her, her tongue swiping out to part Merritt's, the bourbon and sugar mixing together all over again.

Dylan pressed her back against the counter, and Merritt met her inch for inch, her hips remembering the rhythm. Their movements began to shift toward frantic as Dylan lifted her by the thighs, setting her on the counter beside the stove. Merritt's dark curls fell around them as she leaned her face down to continue kissing Dylan, her fingers moving over the woman's strong jaw, the softness of the short fuzz of her undercut, the cords in her neck and muscles in her shoulders. Memories of last Christmas flooded Merritt's mind, particularly the night that Dylan made her orgasm so many times she forgot her own name. Memories be damned, because why think about the past when the present was so much better— Dylan's hands gripped her thighs, their breaths coming faster now.

She was suddenly thankful they were alone in the house— the Vanlaninghams were out at Kellen's mother's house, and Rebekah had driven to Salida to see her daughter. If Dylan wanted to spread her out on the counter and feast on her right there, who was she to stop her? At least they'd have privacy.

A charred smell brought her back down to earth and she turned to see the bourbon and sugar mix burning on the stove.

"Oh fuck," Dylan said, stepping away from her. She turned off the burner and lifted the saucepan, moving it to the far counter. "You said you wouldn't burn it."

"I don't think I can be held responsible for that," Merritt joked.

The absence of Dylan pressed against her gave Merritt a chance to catch her breath. She straightened her shirt and watched the chef move in the kitchen, graceful and purposeful. She remembered the last day they'd spent together the year before, making a meal together after Merritt had asked for the recipe of the chicken thighs and mashed potato dinner. Dylan had wrapped her arms around Merritt, steering her arms like Merritt had never held a spatula before. She'd turned to kiss the underside of Dylan's jaw and said, "I could get used to this." And Dylan had smiled back down at her and said, "Me too."

But she'd never really meant that, had she? And had she really thought that Merritt hadn't meant it, either?

And now, as her heart rate slowed and steadied and she was able to think clearly again, she couldn't help but realize what a mistake she was making. She'd spent an entire year piecing her heart and dignity back together, and now she was going to throw away all of that hard work? For what—one week of pleasure?

She slipped off the counter, straightening her top that had twisted in Dylan's skilled hands.

Dylan turned back, then paused. She must have seen the look on Merritt's face. "What's wrong?"

"I don't want this," Merritt said. But she hadn't said the rest of what she really meant: I don't want this to hurt me.

A look of disbelief passed over Dylan's face, but was gone in a moment. She shrugged, relaxing back into her usual posture of casual and calm. "Alright." How she could be so completely unaffected was beyond Merritt.

Merritt wanted to explain. To talk things out. To figure out where they stood and where they could stand in the future. But Dylan's 'whatever' attitude was enraging. Thank god for burning bourbon.

Speaking of, she grabbed her glass and stalked out of the room. Maybe some distance would do her good and let her clear her mind. She walked into the family room, which opened to a long hallway that led down to Huxley's room. The more formal sitting room and Julia and Kellen's room was on the other end of the house, or what they called The North Wing.

She sipped her bourbon, letting her fingers trail along the garlands that hung on every surface in sight. Rebekah had really outdone herself this year. It was gorgeous. And that's just what she needed—a gorgeous distraction from that other gorgeous distraction in the kitchen. She sank into one of the soft leather couches and stared at the glistening lights on the tree as she sipped the warming drink, letting it soothe her aching heart.

MERRITT STARTLED AWAKE at the touch of someone's hand on her arm. Julia stood over her, and as she looked around and realized she must have fallen asleep on the couch in the family room. She had a throw blanket over her that she didn't remember grabbing.

"Hey hon, why don't you go off to bed?" Julia said in her kind mom voice, patting Merritt's shoulder.

Merritt rubbed at her eyes. "Do you need help putting Huxley down?"

Julia shook her head. "He fell asleep in the car and didn't wake up when Kellen carried him in."

"Did you have fun at the in-laws?" Merritt asked, wishing

she had a glass of water. The bourbon had made her wake up with a seriously dry mouth and a slight headache. Or maybe that was from skipping dinner. Ugh, she didn't even want to think of food at a time like this.

"As much fun as you can have with people who vote conservative and want to talk about Ayn Rand," she said, rolling her eyes.

Merritt chuckled. "Fair enough."

"Did you have a good day off?" Julia asked, unwinding the scarf around her neck. They must have just gotten home.

Merritt shrugged. "Yeah, it was relaxing," she lied.

Julia nodded. "I'm glad. Now, go on to bed. You're gonna need your strength, because I might have accidentally promised Huxley he could go to an all-day ice hockey thing with his friends in town in a couple of days, and it's sure to be a very boring day of watching young kids fall down on ice." Her eyes widened as her smile tightened into an apologetic look.

"No worries. It'll be a good time to catch up on some reading," she said.

"Oh, that reminds me. I left a book on the table near the back door for you. Just finished it and thought you'd like it," Julia said, picking up the empty bourbon glass from the table as she walked back toward the kitchen. "Have a good night, Mer."

Merritt called out similar sentiments, then walked to the back door to brave the cold walk to the carriage house. On the table was the book Julia had mentioned, some new research on emotional processing in children under the age of five. Merritt smiled to herself—it was a nice perk of having a professor as an employer. They always had interesting things to talk about, at least, and Julia had always been concerned about Merritt keeping up with current ideas, even out of school. One of the first books Julia had given her had sparked her interest in early childhood emotions in the first place, and she'd wanted to research more ever since.

She examined the book as she hurried across the back lawn, typing in her keycode to the door and stepping inside. The lights were off in the entryway—she'd forgotten to check what time it was. She kicked off her boots and walked down the hallway to find that a lamp was left on in the living area, and below it sat a bowl of mac and cheese.

Even after she'd had to reject Dylan for the sake of not losing herself again, that woman was still concerned for her appetite. Ridiculous. She ate quickly as she flipped through the book, then made her way into the bedroom after brushing her teeth and wrapping her hair in a loose bun to protect her curls. It was pitch black, the curtain pulled tight even against the moonless night. Dylan was sprawled out in bed, fighting what looked like a losing battle with the top sheet in her sleep. She changed into her pajamas in their room, since Dylan was asleep and couldn't see her, then crawled into bed.

"You okay?" Dylan asked softly, and Merritt glanced sideways, though she couldn't make anything out in the dark.

"Yeah," Merritt said quickly. A lie, but not a bad one.

There was a long silence that stretched between them, and Merritt was wondering if Dylan had fallen asleep when she finally said, "What was up with you in the kitchen?" Her voice seemed to catch as she spoke, cracking just slightly in a way that made Merritt flinch.

She could answer her. She could explain her feelings. She could put herself out of her misery.

And if she did that, she opened herself to more heartbreak.

She couldn't chance it. She couldn't do that to herself again. She'd spent so much time resenting Dylan for never calling last year that she couldn't spend another year going through that. If not just for herself, then for Ezra and Kylie, who had to hear about it nonstop for an embarrassing amount of time.

She didn't say anything, hoping that Dylan would think she was asleep. The silence flooded the room like a fog, obscuring what was right before her. The blankets from Dylan's bed rustled, and she let out a breath knowing that Dylan had finally fallen asleep.

Then, her bed shifted, and she felt Dylan sitting beside her. She startled, pushing onto her elbows.

"I care about you, Merritt," Dylan said, her voice soft as falling snow. The woman wasn't touching her, wasn't forcing her way through the very sturdy boundary that Merritt kept up at all times. She was merely there, and saying exactly the right thing. But how in the world could Merritt trust her again?

She wanted to believe her. She really did. But how could they ever get past the past? How was she meant to open up the floodgates of her heart without a way to close them again? Her mouth remained tightly closed as she looked up into the darkness toward Dylan. She couldn't see much, but she knew the shape of her. The broadness of her shoulders, the muscles that ran down her back, the color that spread over her pale skin in beautiful designs. She knew the full shape of her; that shape had stayed imprinted on Merritt for a year.

"I know it takes you a while to come around, but I'll be here when you do," Dylan whispered. Then, she stood again and climbed back into her own bed, judging from the sound of the blankets moving.

Merritt laid back, staring up into the darkness above her head. Had she dreamt that or had that really happened?

"Oh, and Merry Christmas," Dylan added.

"Merry Christmas," Merritt answered, her throat tight with emotion.

CHAPTER 8

DYLAN

W as making a last-minute and elaborate pumpkin pie a mistake? It was. Dylan was *not* a baker. But would it taste absolutely delicious and be the perfect end to the perfect meal? She sure as hell hoped so.

In times of intense stress, cooking had always calmed her. Now, it became a vicious cycle when she was stressed about cooking to… cook more. But she was trying something new, hoping it would impress Merritt, at least.

She tested the pumpkin ganache to see if it was firm, then piped whipped cream in rosettes. She was terrible at pastry and wished idly that Merritt had been there to help her over this one last hurdle. She'd spent nearly the entire day wishing Merritt was there with her, but she was spending time with the Vanlaninghams, as far as Dylan knew.

How had yesterday gone so awry so quickly? She thought they were finally on the same page, and the way Merritt was kissing her made it seem like they were in agreement. Merritt's soft body pressed tightly to hers, those full, dark lips parting just for her. But just as quickly as Merritt had let her guard down, it had come right back up. What had happened in the thirty seconds when she pulled the smoking bourbon off of the burner? She'd been racking her mind all day to figure out where she'd gone wrong.

She knew what she had done right, at least, and that was giving Merritt her space. She'd found her asleep on the couch and pulled a throw blanket over her, then left a late-night snack out for her at the carriage house for when she'd returned. If she did at all.

But where had she gone so wrong?

Dylan shook her head. She couldn't get distracted. She had caramel and pumpkin ganache pies with streusel toppings to finish. She'd made it this far and would soon begin serving dessert to the family, of which there was an overwhelming amount. She'd always thought that Emily and Richard Gilmore were hyperbolic archetypes, but their doppelgängers were sitting in the dining room she was about to enter.

She added the streusel, then turned to take the chocolate bourbon tart out of the refrigerator, along with the Kentucky Derby pie she'd whipped up earlier that morning. Rebekah appeared across the kitchen island, her stern eyebrows raised. "They're ready for dessert."

"Why do they suddenly think we're their waiters?" Dylan quipped, rolling her eyes.

Rebekah gave her a look that all but said, 'Shut your mouth.'

Dylan's feet ached as she walked into the dining room, plastering on a large smile. "Dessert time," she said enthusiastically. The Vanlaninghams were paying her a pretty penny for that enthusiasm and talent, and so she'd give it to them. She described the pies, looking around the table at the Vanlaningham extended family, with Julia and Kellen at the center, Emily and Richard Gilmore at either end, a bowtied and slick-haired Huxley seated near his grandmother. Kellen's sister, her husband, and their son were on the other side of the table, and judging by everyone's plates, the feast had been a success. Like any good chef, she eyed the leftovers, ideas for remixes of meals for the coming days playing out in her head. "How was everyone's meal? What else can I get for you?"

Kellen's father, whose name was undoubtedly something like Archibald, raised his wine glass. "I'll have another," he said, not even looking at her.

"Of course," she said, reaching for the wine bottle that was literally right in front of him.

Rebekah tidied up the large platters and Dylan reached out to take them from her hands and carry them back into the kitchen.

Merritt sat at the kitchen counter, tipping some of the tiny meat pie appetizers onto a plate. Even in sweatpants and an oversized sweatshirt, her hair pulled back in a messy bun with a few loose curls around her face, she was stunning. Her dark, wide eyes turned to Dylan in surprise, like she'd just been caught stealing.

"Here, let me make you a plate," Dylan offered, setting down the platters and finding a plate in the cupboard, even as Merritt protested. "It's Christmas, so you have to let people do nice things for you."

"Is that so?"

"Yeah, it's the number one rule of Christmas."

"I thought it was the other way around, like you're supposed to do nice things for other people," Merritt said, settling onto one of the counter height bar stools.

"Well, in that case, then it's my plan to do something nice for someone else. You'd ruin *my* Christmas if you didn't let me," Dylan teased, serving up pork, hasselback potatoes au gratin, roasted carrots in ginger sauce, roasted Brussels sprouts with pickled shallots, and fresh bread rolls.

"Can I get more of the carrots? They look really good," Merritt said, pointing.

"Expertly peeled, if I do say so myself," Dylan smirked. She added more carrots to Merritt's plate, then tossed it in the microwave to warm up.

"How was your day?" Merritt asked, her hands properly folded on the counter like she was conducting a business interview.

"It's been busy. I think I'm going to clean up after dessert, grab a glass of wine, and take a bath with CBD epsom salts, a bath bomb or two, and Grey's Anatomy playing on my phone," Dylan confessed. Detailed, sure, but she'd been dreaming of a long soak in the tub since her feet started hurting around mid-afternoon.

"Sounds nice," Merritt said, reaching for the plate as Dylan handed it to her. Her eyes lit up at the heaping pile of food, and Dylan felt something tug deep in her chest at the delight on her face. The woman had been telling her all week that her food was fine, okay, and needed more salt, but had somehow found it in her heart to eat impressive amounts of it none-theless. Hidden couch mashed potatoes included.

"What about you? How are you closing out Christmas?" Dylan asked.

"Hopefully in a food coma," Merritt said, shoveling Brus-sels sprouts into her mouth. "Spent the day watching Huxley receive gifts more expensive than the GDP of a small country, and that really takes it out of you. Gotta replenish the tank."

Dylan laughed and began working through the dishes as they sat in comfortable silence. She finished up with the platters and collected the dessert dishes so that Rebekah wouldn't have to clean anything in the dining room or kitchen. When she came back into the room, Merritt was still sitting at the counter, reading a book and drinking a glass of tea. Dylan offered her a slice of pie and she groaned that she was too full, but still accepted a tiny sliver of each type.

Merritt continued to read as she ate the pie, and Dylan couldn't help but imagine this was what life could be like with her. Simple, companionable. They hadn't had this type of connection last year. Dylan would slip into the carriage house at night and they'd spend those hours wisely, but they never just sat together, enjoying one another. Dylan had shown her how to cook a meal that she had raved about, but that's kind of where it stuttered out—it was passion, but it was not intimacy.

She had kissed nearly every inch of Merritt's body, but sitting together in silence as she did the dishes and Merritt read? Now that felt like intimacy. She had to admit, she liked that idea. She smiled, drying off the decorative platter from the Brussels sprouts, and glanced up to see Merritt looking at her quizzically.

"What's got you in such a good mood?" Merritt asked, standing up to take her empty plate to the dishwasher beside Dylan.

"Do you want to go on a walk?" Dylan asked, drying the last of the casserole dishes.

"Right now?" Merritt asked, looking around.

"Yeah, you know, just around the neighborhood," Dylan said. "Get the circulation moving after so much food."

Merritt tugged on the elastic waist of her sweatpants. "That might be a good idea."

After a few moments of gathering coats, scarves, mittens, and snow boots, they were sufficiently bundled up enough to leave the house on a winter's night. Their boots crunched in the thin layer of snow coating the ground as they made their way down the drive. The Vanlaningham's holiday house was set up on a hill overlooking the small town of Snowy Springs, and the neighborhood lots were large enough to give a semblance of privacy, but not so large that they were walking down some kind of empty country road.

"My family used to drive around at Christmas and look at lights," Dylan said, tucking her chin down into her scarf. The wind bit at her cheeks, the air smelling of cold and pine and woodburning stoves.

"That sounds really nice, actually," Merritt said, shivering and sniffling.

Dylan looped Merritt's arm through hers, pulling her closer. "I think it's my only nice memory of Christmas. They didn't believe in getting me Christmas gifts, though. It's not like I'm mad about not getting presents, but it made me feel so othered in school to not get anything when everyone was bragging about new bikes or Hot Wheels or video games."

She felt Merritt's eyes on her in the dark. "I'm so sorry to hear that. That sounds really awful. Was that choice driven by religion or economics?"

"Just general apathy, I guess," Dylan said, rolling her eyes.

"Did you get birthday presents?" Merritt asked gently.

Dylan scoffed. "No. My mom bought herself a present on my birthday, because she claimed it was a day to honor her giving birth to me, not me being born. Like I had a choice in the matter of being born."

Merritt's hand rubbed Dylan's upper arm. "That's fucked up."

"It is, isn't it?" Dylan said, pausing as they passed a house decked to the nines with Christmas lights and decor. Every tree, every shrub, every line of the roof—covered in lights. "The local airport must have had to issue a warning about this place."

"Can you imagine being the closest neighbor? It'd be like a case of Alaska's midnight sun all December long," Merritt joked.

Dylan laughed, and they continued walking, turning at the end of the winding road to return home.

"I'm fucking freezing," Merritt admitted.

Dylan nodded, laughing. "Same. I can't feel my toes."

They picked up their pace, shuffling along together arm-in-arm down the road, making a few comments about the lights on the houses they passed, and the glow of the small town once they crested the small hill in the middle of the road.

"What about you? What was Christmas like for your family?" Dylan asked.

Merritt's breath fogged in front of her as she let out a slow exhale. "Well, a lot of mouths to feed. We didn't have much, but we got things we needed, like socks. I always got socks. Christmas with that many kids was chaos, though, so even with very few presents, it felt like a big deal. One year I got some off-brand Barbie dollhouse that I absolutely loved and cherished for way too long, though. It was a hand-me-down from a relative, I later learned, but I loved that thing."

"That makes sense that you were a dollhouse kid. Always loved taking care of others," Dylan observed. "Or maybe just being in charge and bossing people around."

Merritt scoffed. "It's not my fault that I just know better."

"Did your relationship with your family fray because of religion?" Dylan tried to gently ask.

"Politics, technically," Merritt said, shrugging. "They weren't very cool about me coming out, but I really lost them to Fox News years ago. My siblings and I were never close enough to bother keeping in touch, I guess. And if you think I'm bossy, my mom is an absolute tyrant."

"Ah, one of those her-way-or-the-highway type of people?" Dylan asked.

Merritt sighed. "Yep. And nothing was ever good enough."

"Ah, I know that one well," Dylan said, shaking her head. She held up a hand as if making a toast with an invisible champagne glass. "Here's to surviving our childhoods against all odds."

Merritt raised an invisible glass as well, cheersing hers. "And to lifelong trauma."

Dylan laughed, the macabre toast just the right kind of dark humor for her taste. "And to therapy."

"Oh yeah, I'm pouring one out for all of the therapists who have to deal with our bullshit," Merritt said, miming tipping a bottle.

They paused as they came back to the holiday house—the reprieve from the workplace felt like they'd been gone for much longer than just twenty minutes. It was as though the further she got Merritt away from the house, the more open she'd been. It felt like she'd trapped lightning in a bottle— how could she keep Merritt this open?

Merritt sniffled again, shivering as she picked up the pace to skirt around the main house and walk directly to the carriage house. Dylan followed her inside, quickly shutting the door behind them as they pulled off their coats and tried to clap and stomp feeling back into their hands and feet.

Merritt fussed with the zipper on her coat, tugging force-fully but getting nowhere. Dylan reached out and clicked the zipper back onto its track, then slowly lowered the zipper pull, opening the coat. Such a simple, innocent act, and yet, as her hands moved lower, peeling back the layer of clothing, something in the air seemed to warm between them. Merritt's breathing hitched, and Dylan could tell she felt it, too.

She had a crazy idea. She helped pull off Merritt's snow boots and kicked off her own, then took Merritt by the hand, leading her down the hallway towards the bathroom. The woman's dark eyes stared into hers, questioning but not resisting.

"I know a way to get warm quickly," Dylan said, a grin pulling at the corner of her mouth.

"Dylan," Merritt said, her voice a warning.

Dylan reached to plug the bathtub drain, then turn on the warm water. The large tub began to fill, and Dylan reached over her shoulders to tug her shirt over her head, revealing a sports bra. It was a gamble of a move—this kind of forwardness had scared Merritt off before.

Merritt looked from the tub back to Dylan. "You're taking a bath?"

"We're taking a bath," Dylan corrected.

Merritt's eyebrows raised in surprise. "Oh, are we?" Still, her eyes raked over Dylan's shoulders and torso.

"No funny business. Just two people getting warm and relaxing after a hard day."

"Two people getting naked," Merritt snorted.

Dylan held out a pinky. "I promise not to make a move on you in the vulnerable state of bathing."

Merritt hooked her pinky through Dylan's, then rubbed her hands together, flexing her fingers, and looked down to the water. "Was this your plan all along? To get me frostbitten enough to agree to this?"

Dylan couldn't help but chuckle, even if it wasn't true. "What if it was? A good plan, right?"

Merritt smirked, pulling her sweatshirt over her head. "A mastermind, I see."

Dylan's heart skipped a beat, seeing Merritt in just a bralette, the green fabric contrasted against her olive skin. Dylan reached to feel the water to avoid her impulse to reach out and touch Merritt instead. Out of her peripheral vision, she could see Merritt tug her sweatpants over her hips.

"Nothing you haven't seen before, after all," Merritt muttered, then shimmied out of her underwear and bra, climbing into the water slowly. She hissed that it was a bit hot, but then slapped Dylan's hand away from adjusting the temperature.

Dylan followed suit, discarding her clothes and climbing into the tub to lean against the opposite end. Merritt's legs on either side of hers, their knees and shoulders above water, but the rest distorted under the ripple of water.

Just feeling Merritt's naked body beside her own was enough to set every nerve in her body into overdrive. Her heightened awareness of every inch of skin that slid against her own was distracting, and they sat in the quiet together, either lost in their own thoughts or too afraid to break the easy silence.

"I do believe the guidebook said wine was available in the bathtub," Merritt said finally, shaking her head. "I'm going to have to knock a star off my Yelp review of this place for the oversight."

Dylan laughed. "You're right, I did say wine and a bath, didn't I?" She stood quickly, grabbing a towel, and heard Merritt gasp.

"I was joking. You don't have to get out to grab wine," she protested as Dylan hurried out of the bathroom and ran to the kitchenette to grab a previously opened wine bottle from the counter and two glasses from the drying rack. Merritt was laughing as Dylan hurried back, not bothering to set anything down before climbing back in the bath. "You are ridiculous."

"What my baby wants, my baby gets," Dylan teased before she could think better of it, and she could feel Merritt stiffen beside her at the nickname. "I just mean, I can't afford another two star review. We're trying for five here."

Dylan set down the glasses on the edge of the tub and pulled the cork out of the bottle with her teeth, spitting it onto the floor. She poured the wine, handing Merritt a glass. "There you go, Miss Perkins. Please reconsider your customer satisfaction survey. Your ultimate pleasure is our goal."

Merritt choked on her wine, but was grinning when she pulled away from the glass, wiping at the corners of her mouth.

They chatted and joked about nothing of importance until the wine bottle was empty and their cheeks were glowing with warmth even as the water began to grow tepid. Maybe it was the wine, or the comfort between them, or the growing tension, but she noticed they were moving closer and closer together, their legs rubbing against one another's, their hands grazing each other's bodies more and more.

How does one melt an iceberg? Warm water, of course.

After they compared pruned fingers, they decided it was time to climb out of the bath. Dylan handed Merritt a towel, then wrapped herself in one, reaching for her toothbrush. Merritt grabbed her own, and they watched each other in the mirror as they brushed their teeth, taking turns spitting out toothpaste and rinsing their mouths. Dylan carried the wine glasses to the sink and tossed the bottle in the recycling bin.

When she returned to the bedroom, she found that the lights were dimmed and Merritt was already lying in bed. She walked to the edge of her bed to find the pajamas she'd stuffed under her pillow, and turned to see Merritt lifting the edge of her blankets and reaching out a hand. Dylan paused, one million questions popping into her mind. Since when had Merritt taken the lead on anything that even remotely put them in the realm of friends? Friends that took baths together and apparently climbed into bed naked with one another...

"No funny business," Merritt said. "I was just thinking, it's Christmas, and it'd be nice to... you know, just... not be alone?" She looked up at Dylan, her eyes so wide and vulnerable. Dylan's brain went completely blank and her good sense was gone. Forgetting any reason why this might be a bad idea, she dropped her towel to the ground and moved to climb into the tiny twin size bed, settling beside Merritt.

"No funny business, even though you have requested naked cuddling," she repeated back, even as her hand found Merritt's bare waist, their legs rubbing against one another's.

"Exactly," Merritt said.

They shifted until Merritt's head rested on Dylan's shoulder, tucked in against her side, her face literal inches from Dylan's breasts. They fit together like puzzle pieces, and the feel of her was so familiar. She was almost too afraid to move, afraid to break the spell or spook Merritt. Eventually, Merritt's breathing went even, and Dylan felt like she could breathe again, and before long, she couldn't help but be pulled into a deep and dreamless sleep, held in the arms of a woman she cared about.

CHAPTER 9

Merritt would never again underestimate how boring it was to support a child in sports. As Huxley wobbled around on the ice with a gaggle of other kids steadying himself on his hockey stick, she sat in a cold metal flip-down chair in the stands along the side.

Thank goodness she'd brought her laptop. Open on her browser was the NYU Steinhardt application for the Developmental Psychology doctoral program. She had everything ready except for her statement of purpose and the letter of recommendation from Julia.

The deadline to apply was January 1, and she felt disheartened by the idea of asking Julia for such a quick turnaround on the recommendation letter. She couldn't even admit to Julia that she was thinking about her PhD, much less admit to her that she was already in the process of applying for it.

And now, when she was finishing this absolutely critical application on a tight deadline, all she could think about was last night with Dylan. The bath, sleeping next to her… She was so worried she'd wake up grinding herself on Dylan, but she'd slept so soundly. Dylan hadn't flailed around for the first time in a week, and Merritt had woken up feeling excited.

It'd been a long time since she'd been excited about much—but now she was excited about the possibility of her future. From pursuing her doctorate to figuring things out with Dylan, she was eager and ready to see it unfold.

She'd gotten up early that morning, sliding out of bed beside a very naked and very snuggly Dylan, and sat on the couch in her bathrobe, organizing all of her files and documents that she'd been slowly accumulating—her CV, transcripts, and a rough statement of purpose that she'd been revising for weeks. She'd tried to get the small printer in the carriage house working to print out the statement of purpose for better editing with a pen while she waited for Hux the Hockey Star, but hadn't been able to figure it out. Hence, the laptop and the blank page before her. Maybe if she couldn't get that draft right, it was time to just start over.

"You're the Vanlaningham's nanny, right?" a woman asked to her left.

Merritt glanced over to see a slightly familiar woman around her age. She smiled politely. "I am, yeah. Merritt," she said, reaching out a hand to shake.

"Claudia," the woman said by way of introduction. "I'm the Jacobs' nanny."

Ah, maybe that's what it was. Huxley had briefly entertained a friendship with the Jacobs kid but had later told Merritt that he didn't enjoy the way Otis only talked about himself. Merritt tried not to grin at the memory. "Nice to meet you," Merritt said, really hoping that Claudia didn't think they were going to chat it up. This ranked second in terrible social interactions only to being stuck on a plane next to a chatty person who wanted to tell you about their life story. She quickly looked back to her computer, pretending to type a sentence.

"Can I ask you kind of a weird question?" Claudia asked, moving over a seat until she was only one chair away.

Merritt briefly entertained the idea of saying no, but didn't, given that it'd likely be ignored, anyway. "Sure, what's up?"

"Did the Vanlaninghams hire a private chef this year?" Claudia asked, and Merritt went stone-still, anticipation and nerves eating at her.

"Yeah, why?" She asked as politely as she could, even though she could hear the edge in her own voice. Why did she feel so jealous that this woman was talking about Dylan? She had no claim to Dylan and no right to be jealous in the first place.

"The Jacobs had this great chef two years ago, but then your family hired her last year, and I've been wondering what happened to her ever since. Dylan, right?" Claudia explained.

Merritt's mouth went dry as she nodded. "That's the one," she said, trying to appear like she didn't care.

"Pardon me saying so, but we had kind of a thing," Claudia said.

Merritt wanted to throw up. Jealousy, green and ugly, filled her body, drowning out every other emotion. She didn't want to picture Dylan with someone else, and didn't want someone else to be pining over Dylan. Didn't want to picture this woman's hands tangled in Dylan's blonde hair as Dylan —nope. No. She would stop herself there. She settled for an unimpressed nod. "Okay?"

"Do you know if she's still single? She, like, never returned my calls."

Merritt turned to have a good look at Claudia. The woman was younger than she'd previously assumed, had perfectly fluffed chestnut brown hair, clear skin, and a tight sweater that showed off her curves. She couldn't even fault Dylan for being interested. Claudia was a babe.

"Maybe you could put in a good word for me?" Claudia added.

"Uh..." Merritt had a few ideas of the kind of words she'd put in, but none of them were good. She couldn't be mad at Claudia—she clearly had no idea what went on between Merritt and Dylan, and she was just shooting her shot. Still, the emotions that had begun roiling inside of Merritt were not happy or calm. Why was she feeling so affected by Claudia's claims? Despite all her efforts, she liked Dylan, and the thought of losing her again made her sick with worry.

"Don't get me wrong. We never even, like, kissed. But I always felt there was something there," Claudia said.

Merritt paused in her internal rampage, turning toward Claudia again. That was a promising statement. "So when you say 'had a thing' you mean it was a bit one-sided on your part?" she clarified.

Claudia flinched, as though she hadn't expected Merritt to question her. "Well, yeah, but the vibes—"

Huxley squawked loudly and she turned to see him fall on the ice in a grand display of flailing limbs and yelps. Merritt shut her laptop, standing up quickly to see if he was alright or if she needed to intervene. He laid on the ground with his arms spread, completely still. Here she was, getting jealous of some woman she didn't know, filling her head with thoughts of Dylan, when she should have been paying more attention to Huxley. That was her job, not trying to make a player like Dylan put down roots.

She hastily shoved her laptop into her bag while calling out, "Hux, you okay, bud?" When she received no answer and watched the coach and the rest of the boys circle Huxley on the ground, she hopped over the row of chairs in front of her and ran to the edge of the ice. Her tall block-heeled boots were probably not the best option for ice, but she wasn't about to just wait and see if Hux was okay. She shuffled on the ice, sliding and slipping, but made it over to Huxley without falling on her ass. Somehow. Probably thanks to pure adrenaline and panic.

The coach shoved his hands in the pockets of his track jacket. "He's alright." Yeah, well, she would see for herself now, wouldn't she?

"You okay, bud?" she asked again, kneeling beside him to get a better look.

"What are you doing?" He stared up at her through the grate of his helmet. "I'm alright. Just knocked the wind out of me."

The boys surrounding Huxley were getting restless and began skating away, their blades slicing through the ice with hisses of metal. Even the coach had walked away, calling something out to the group.

"I'm *fine*, Merritt. You didn't need to run out here," Huxley said, pushing himself up on his elbows. "So embarrassing."

"Well, that's what you get for not answering me," Merritt said.

"I'm not a baby. I don't need you to baby me," he continued.

"Noted, my dude." Merritt reached down for his elbow to pull him up, but he pulled out of her grasp.

"I can do it," he snapped.

She held up her hands in surrender and waited as he rolled around like a flipped turtle. Eventually, he got a hand under himself and pushed himself up, then into a kneeling position. He was panting with effort, but in all fairness, so was she.

"Actually my butt kinda hurts. Can we go home?" He said it so quietly she could barely hear him.

She tried not to smile. He was becoming so fiercely independent that she did enjoy the moments where he needed her, even a little. "Of course. I'm hungry anyway."

"Me too," he agreed as she stood and he regained his balance. He cleared his throat and announced to the other kids, "She says we have to go home." He sighed for dramatic effect.

A laugh bubbled up in her chest at the way he was able to look so put out by something that was his own idea. Ah, she did not miss being a kid with appearances to keep up.

After a very slow and careful shuffle off the ice to the tune of multiple adolescent boys complaining about her ruining their game—Huxley included—she drove them home, as requested.

J ULIA WAS SITTING in the living room near the entry of the main house when they walked in. Huxley was walking like he'd just ridden a horse for four days, and Julia looked from the kid back up to her with a question in her eyes. She knew Julia well enough to know that the thought behind it was, 'Do I even want to ask?'

"I think he bruised his tailbone," Merritt explained. "Why don't you go shower and change into some comfortable clothes so we can lay around the rest of the day?"

Huxley giggled at the opportunity. "Yeah, my butt needs a relaxing break."

"If I had a nickel for every time I thought the exact same thing," Merritt said, dropping her bag by the bench in the foyer as Huxley hurried out of the room.

Julia watched her in a way that made her instantly paranoid, like Julia knew something she didn't. Her time with the Vanlaninghams had been long enough that she'd gotten to know their ticks and quirks—Kellen fussed with his clothing when he was uncomfortable, tugging on his collar and sleeves. Julia just watched her, like a cat watching a mouse— not prey, exactly, but the sheer confidence of knowing what will happen in the end.

Anxiety clung to every fiber of Merritt's being as she forced a casual tone. "You were right. Ice hockey was so boring," she said, hanging her scarf on a coat hook. "Zero fist fights."

"What even is hockey without fist fights?" Julia joked along with her, which did something to soothe the anxious ache under her sternum.

"It's just sloppy figure skating at that point, right?" Merritt said, shrugging.

She walked into the living room, a room she'd rarely spent time in since being at the holiday house. The formal nature of the sofas and chairs circled around for quiet conversation unnerved her in a way she couldn't put her finger on. She much preferred the long sectional of the family room where she wasn't worried about somehow breaking the furniture if she sat down too quickly.

"Do you need anything?" she asked Julia, glancing around. With Huxley getting older and more independent and less likely to try to constantly put himself in harm's way, she'd somehow morphed into Julia and Kellen's nanny as much as his.

That's when she saw it. A paper on the coffee table. The pounding of her heart threatened to drown out any other noise in the room. Somehow, Julia had found her statement of purpose.

She could have acted like she had never seen it before. She could have just owned it and confessed right there on the spot, begging for forgiveness. But neither of those seemed right, exactly, and she didn't know why. Neither option seemed fair to Julia and everything the Vanlaninghams had done for her.

"I think you left this on the printer this morning," Julia said, sipping her tea, then setting down the cup with painstaking slowness.

"I must have," Merritt said, taking a deep breath. She folded her hands together to stop them from shaking. "Julia—"

She was cut off by the movement of Julia standing up and wrapping her arms around Merritt. "You're finally doing it!" she exclaimed.

Surprise muddled all of Merritt's thoughts. This was not exactly how she'd thought the conversation would go. "Wh-what?"

"You're finally applying to a PhD program!" Julia repeated, holding her by the shoulders. The older woman's eyes crinkled at the edges as she pulled Merritt in for another hug. "I never wanted to pressure you into it, but I'm so relieved you've finally started."

Laughter released all of the anxious pressure built up in Merritt's chest and she hugged Julia back. "I... wasn't expecting this kind of a response," she admitted.

"Are you kidding me? I feel like I've been dropping hints for three years, Mer," Julia said, sitting back down on the couch. She grabbed her glasses from beside the printed out paper. "I do want to go over this with you, though. I think we could make it stronger."

Merritt sat down carefully on the sofa beside Julia, wonderment delaying her ability to process her thoughts. "You're not mad at all?"

"Why would I be mad?" Julia asked, her tone confused.

"Because I wouldn't be Huxley's nanny anymore," Merritt began.

Julia waved a hand in the air dismissively. "Don't be ridiculous. He hasn't needed a full-time nanny for awhile now. We just all love you too much to let you go," she said.

An emotional lump lodged in Merritt's throat. "That's really kind of you to say," she croaked. "And in that same vein, I was wondering if you'd be able to—and I know it's really last minute, so feel free to tell me no, because I know these things take time—and if you say no I won't be upset, I really do understand—"

"I've had a letter of recommendation ready for you for

months, if that's what you're about to ask," Julia said, looking at her over the edge of the statement of purpose in her hand. "And I hope you'll consider Dr. Singh's lab at NYU." Merritt nodded enthusiastically. "Now. Let's talk about this opening paragraph."

CHAPTER 10

Dylan

Dylan glanced up from the counter of the kitchenette as Merritt walked in just as the sun was setting. She'd been leaning against it, playing on her phone, trying to distract herself. She cleared out of her text messages and slipped her phone back in her pocket. Dylan had spent her afternoon off trying to avoid thinking about the night before, the way being around Merritt made her feel solid and whole. Her nervous energy had culminated in making an elaborate new meal out of leftovers for Kellen to warm up for dinner, since the Vanlaninghams had given her the afternoon and evening off to rest after the marathon of the Christmas Day feast.

Merritt groaned, kicking off her boots haphazardly by the sound of it. She walked into the living area carrying her laptop and a few sheets of paper that looked like they'd gotten in an epic battle with a red pen.

The realization hit her that Merritt walking in through that door felt a lot like Merritt coming home. And she liked that. A lot.

"Beer?" Dylan asked.

"Yes, dear god, please," Merritt said, setting down her things on the coffee table, then flopping onto the couch. Her curls were tied back in a messy bun. "And then no critical thinking for the rest of the day."

Dylan grabbed a beer and walked into the living area to hand it to Merritt. "Movie?"

"Sure."

"Popcorn?"

Merritt grinned, looking up at her. "I do have a bone to pick with you," she said.

"A bone?" Dylan asked, shoving her hands awkwardly in the pockets of her jeans.

"Yeah, I met this woman today," Merritt began, and Dylan tried to keep a straight face until she could tell where this was going. "Does the name Claudia ring any bells?"

Her eyebrow quirked in confusion. "Not really."

"Were you a private chef for the Jacobs family?" Merritt continued, her grin growing more mischievous.

She nodded, but didn't see the connection.

"I met their nanny, Claudia, today." Merritt said, loudly sipping for effect.

Dylan couldn't picture her face, only the weird way she was *always* lurking around when Dylan was working. She consistently gave Dylan the creeps, frequently touching her arm and laughing way too loud. "I have a vague recollection," she said honestly.

"Well, you sure made an impression on her," Merritt teased. When Dylan frowned, Merritt continued, "She asked me today if you're single."

Dylan's cheeks heated in embarrassment. "What'd you say?"

"I said yes and gave her your number," Merritt said with a wink.

"You didn't," Dylan's stomach plummeted down a flight of

stairs at the thought. She sat down on the couch near Merritt's knees. "Please tell me you didn't."

Merritt looked her over, as if appraising whether or not to give her the real answer. "I didn't. I didn't get the chance, because Huxley fell and then wanted to go home. He's fine."

Dylan's hands slid across her brow as she pretended to wipe sweat away. "A close call."

Merritt laughed,the sound a little too evil in Dylan's opinion. She looked pointedly at the laptop and papers. "Besides that, did you have a good day at least?"

Merritt sighed, puffing her cheeks out. "Julia found out about my doctoral program application," she said, trying to maneuver the beer to her mouth while she laid back against the couch.

"Oh, fuck," Dylan said, running an anxious hand through her hair. "What'd she say?"

Merritt rolled her eyes, chugging from the beer can as she held up a finger to signal that Dylan should wait for the answer. She paused, taking a deep breath, and shook her head. "That's the thing. She said she was waiting for me to do this for a while. She even had my recommendation letter all written. Then she helped me with my statement of purpose."

A surprised laugh caught in Dylan's throat. "That's great news! I feel like we should celebrate," she said. "Want to go out to dinner? There's this cute restaurant here I've been wanting to try but I've never gotten the chance."

Merritt's eyes looked up questioningly as she continued drinking her beer like she was desperately competing in a frat party drinking game. "Like... a date?" She covered her mouth as she hiccuped and burped at the same time. "Oh my god, sorry."

Dylan laughed, grimacing. "I'll drive."

• • •

Clover, the restaurant she'd been dying to try, was just as adorable as she thought it would be. She was geeking out over the menu options as Merritt laughed at her, claiming that she'd never seen anyone get so excited over sunchokes covered in raclette before.

Dylan ordered a truly absurd amount of food, but who could rein themselves in when the options were so good? Who knew that a tiny town like Snowy Springs would have this quality of cuisine?

Dylan raised her Old Fashioned in a toast. "To pursuing your doctorate," she said.

Merritt grinned mischievously. "To furthering ourselves," she said, gently clinking her wine glass against Dylan's lowball glass.

"Ourselves?" Dylan asked.

"Yeah, let's talk about your next steps," Merritt said, sipping the deep red liquid in the glass a little more delicately than she had chugged her beer earlier.

"I thought we weren't critically thinking any more today," Dylan countered. She was happy for Merritt, but she was in no mood to try to figure out her life at the moment. Maybe it could be a New Year's Resolution. Or next year's New Year's Resolution. What was the rush?

"Very funny," Merritt said, tightening her mouth into a thin line like she did when she was considering how to get her way.

They discussed ideas of how she could take the next steps in her career over dinner, pausing to talk about how delicious everything was and share bites of food. Merritt was in such a good mood, and elation bubbled up inside of Dylan at the knowledge that she was some part, however small, of making her happy.

When dinner was over, Dylan pushed her chair back. "I'm going to use the restroom," she said, taking her phone out of her back pocket and placing it on the table. "I have an irrational fear of dropping my phone in a toilet. Let me know if I miss any calls from Claudia?"

Merritt snorted, giving her a thumbs up.

When she returned from the restroom, Merritt had an odd look on her face, pale and shocked, her dark eyes wide and wild.

"What happened?" Sliding into her chair, she reached across the table to touch Merritt's hand. What could possibly have made her look like she'd seen a ghost? "Are you okay? Is Huxley okay?"

Merritt silently slid Dylan's phone across the table, lit up and unlocked. Her mouth went suddenly dry as she saw what was on the screen. She fidgeted with her napkin. "You... went through my phone?"

"What kind of monster doesn't have a passcode?" Merritt said in a harsh whisper. "I saw something about message not being delivered pop up and I was powerless against the curiosity, given that the message was *to me*."

Dylan took a long pull of her Old Fashioned, but didn't feel the need to defend herself. Well, now the truth was out there.

"Why did you never tell me?" Merritt asked, her voice cracking with emotion.

Dylan shrugged, running her fingertips over the cool glass of her drink. "You didn't ask."

"You texted me dozens, if not hundreds of times," Merritt said, her finger scrolling on the screen to reveal all of the messages in green bubbles. Dylan had started in February, knowing that even if Merritt had thought it was casual, she never had. It took her too long to get her courage up to reply to Merritt's first casual text, though, and she was gutted when her first text back popped up green—the realization that Merritt had blocked her was devastating, and she knew that the only chance to convince Merritt to give her another chance was to play it off. No one wanted a desperate heartbroken idiot. Plus, when Merritt did finally unblock her, the messages wouldn't show up for her, and she'd never have to know.

She'd never have to know that every few days for an entire year, Dylan had texted her things like: *I'm watching the sunset and thinking of you* or *Remembering the time you held an ice cube in your teeth and ran it over my bare skin, followed by your warm tongue* and *I miss you miserably, but I can't wait to see you this Christmas.*

Even this week, there were texts that said: *You look so cute in that sweater* and *Wish you'd come back to bed* and *I am crazier for you each and every day.* And then the last one, which she'd sent right before they'd left for dinner: *You're going to fall for me, Merritt Perkins, and I can't wait to catch you.*

"You didn't ghost me," Merritt whispered, shaking her head. "You..." She held her hands over her face. "I'm such an idiot."

"No, you're not," Dylan said, reaching for Merritt's hands to pull them away from her face. "I am. When I sent that first text and you'd already blocked me, I realized I'd waited too long," she confessed. "I'm so sorry for ever making you think that you weren't constantly on my mind, Merritt."

Merritt, trying so hard to look unshakable, burst into tears right at the table, her shoulders shaking as she blubbered, her words entirely unintelligible. Dylan panicked, scrambling around to kneel on the ground beside her.

"Oh my god, is she *proposing*?" a woman at a nearby table exclaimed in perhaps the loudest whisper of all time.

"I think she's proposing," another person said at a table on the opposite side of them.

"I'm not—I'm... It's..." Dylan looked around, several sets of eyes on the two of them. This was something out of a total nightmare, the kind where she showed up somewhere important naked or had forgotten to study for a test. Now she had to add 'Make the woman who you love cry in public and then a bunch of strangers mistake your idiocy for a proposal.' Fantastic. She turned back to Merritt and lowered her voice. "Do you want to get out of here?"

Merritt nodded, wiping at her face and sniffling. "Yes," she said.

"She said yes," the first woman announced, and four tables of couples and families burst into applause nearby.

Dylan couldn't help but laugh at the absurdity of the situation—and thankfully, Merritt seemed to think it was a tiny bit comical as well, because she chuckled as Dylan took her hand and all but ran out of the restaurant before someone from the staff brought them a slice of cake to celebrate their fake engagement.

CHAPTER 11

Merritt wasn't sure who started it, or if they'd just launched themselves at each other simultaneously once Dylan had pulled into the driveway. All she knew was that she was being pressed against the door of the carriage house, Dylan's mouth on hers, warm and tasting of whiskey. Her hands threaded through Dylan's hair, tugging her high, tight bun undone to watch her locks fall in messy waves around her shoulders as she struggled to typed in the key code to the door.

"You're bad at locks the way I'm bad at zippers," Merritt teased. Dylan snorted in amusement, taking Merritt's mouth again as the door unlocked and they finally fell inside.

"Way too many layers," Dylan said against her lips, pulling back to hastily throw her own coat off, then reach for Merritt's zipper.

Merritt's hands fumbled with her coat, and Dylan yanked on it, finally releasing it and pushing it off of Merrit's shoulders.

Dylan claimed Merritt's mouth in a bruising kiss, tugging

Merritt's bottom lip between her teeth as Merritt moaned and clutched her tighter, electric pulses sparking through her entire body.

"I've been thinking about this all year," Dylan murmured against her skin, nipping and sucking at the sensitive places on her neck and collarbones as her fingers dug into Merritt's waist.

"Have you?" Merritt said with a wry smile. "What exactly have you imagined?"

"First, kissing you just like this," Dylan said, her hands cupping Merritt's face as their lips crashed together once more. Dylan guided her backwards, pressing Merritt up against a wall. "And I did have a very clear image of spreading you out on the bed, but…" She paused, looking around, then tugged Merritt towards the living room, their mouths and hands in a frenzy as they stumbled over their steps until Dylan pulled her down onto the couch, Merritt straddling her waist. Dylan gripped her ass through her jeans. "This will have to do."

"Not too shabby," Merritt said, grinding her hips into Dylan's lap.

"Still too many layers," Dylan said, pulling off Merritt's sweater, then unbuttoning her pants. Merritt's own hands were hard at work getting Dylan's shirt unbuttoned and yanked off of her arms.

Dylan paused on the clothing removal to pull Merritt flush against her, and Merritt gasped at the warmth of the press of their skin, her heart pounding as Dylan's mouth found her nipple through the fabric of her bralette.

"Are you sure you want this?" Dylan asked. "I want you to be sure."

"One billion percent sure," Merritt moaned.

Dylan tipped her head back, softness in her eyes and tone as she said, "I haven't been with anyone else since you."

"Really?" Merrit asked, somewhat surprised.

"Really." Dylan said, holding Merritt's entire heart in her hands so gently that Merritt couldn't help but trust her.

She stared down into those green eyes, the eyes of the kindest, sweetest, most infuriating woman she'd ever met. "I haven't been with anyone else either."

She'd waited so long for this, and now that it was happening, she thought her heart might explode from anticipation. Her hands tangled in Dylan's hair as Dylan found her nipple again and she moaned her approval. She was wound so tightly that she was sure she'd come the moment Dylan was between her thighs—tongue, fingers, or otherwise.

Dylan shifted Merritt to the side, moving to cover her as she left a trail of kisses along Merritt's ribs, her stomach, her hips. She tugged Merritt's pants down over her legs as Merritt shimmied out of them the rest of the way. She paused, looking up through her lashes at Merritt, and it occurred to Merritt that she was asking for consent to go further. Merritt smiled and nodded, throwing her forearm over her eyes.

Dylan's hand caught her wrist, and she was shocked at the intensity of Dylan's look when their eyes locked again. "I want you to watch me fuck you." Her voice was a low growl, and Merritt didn't think it was possible, but she grew even more turned on at the command.

She nodded again, and Dylan didn't even bother removing Merritt's underwear before leaning in, pulling the lacy panties to the side, and drawing her tongue over Merritt's clit. Dylan's green eyes stared up at her, holding her stare, daring her to not look away.

Merritt whimpered as Dylan pulled Merritt's legs over her shoulders, opening her wide as Dylan dragged her tongue slowly, taking her time despite Merritt's nearly endless pleas and moans.

Her orgasm wound inside of her lower belly quickly, then exploded in every direction as Dylan licked and sucked, holding on through Merritt's desperate thrashing and cries of pleasure.

Dylan paused only when Merritt was able to take a deep breath again, relaxing back into the pillows. Dylan sat up with a grin, wiping at her mouth.

"Okay, glad that's out of the way," Dylan remarked and Merritt scoffed.

"Excuse me?"

"Because now? Now we can really take our time," Dylan said, and Merritt pulled her close for a kiss.

"And now it's your turn," Merritt said, pushing against Dylan until they tumbled to the floor with laughter and kisses pressed to any bare skin within reach.

Merritt kneeled, pulling off Dylan's pants, then paused, glancing toward the bedroom. "I have an idea."

"I'm all for ideas," Dylan said, pulling her bra over her head and leaning back on her elbows as Merritt ran into the bedroom. She found her vibrator in her suitcase, then hurried back out to the living room.

Dylan laughed as soon as she saw what was in Merritt's hand. "I thought you were going to use that all alone in your very own private room."

"Well, now it's being put to better use," Merritt said, turning the rabbit on. "May I use this on you?"

Dylan nodded quickly, her eyebrows raised in what Merritt could only read as anticipation.

Merritt moved to prop herself up beside Dylan, one hand guiding the vibrator over her nipples as she leaned in to kiss and suck at Dylan's neck, tiny noises of pleasure set loose from the woman's parted lips. Her mouth trailed after the vibrator, taking her time over Dylan's chest, over her ribs, pausing to nip at the swell of softness around her hip bones. "Fuck, you are so sexy," Merritt murmured against her skin, feeling Dylan shudder under her mouth.

She let the vibrator graze over Dylan's Calvin Kleins,

drawing it up and down as Dylan's head tipped back and her hands grasped at the rug beneath them. She moved to bite the waistband of Dylan's underwear, tugging them down as Dylan mouthed the word *fuck* while watching her.

She moved the smaller nub of the rabbit vibrator over Dylan's clit and watched Dylan bite her lip, her hips bucking.

She was surprised as Dylan moved, sitting up and pushing Merritt down onto the ground, taking hold of the vibrator.

"Not fair," Merritt protested.

"I have an idea, too," Dylan smirked. "Can I put this inside of you?"

"I mean, if you must," Merritt said, pretending to sound much more put out about it than she was. "But I really wanted to make you come."

"Well, I want us to come together," Dylan said, sliding the vibrator between Merritt's thighs and into her, until the larger part of the vibrator was all of the way inside and the smaller part was concentrated over her clit.

Merritt arched her back, so sensitive from her earlier orgasm that the vibration almost felt like too much. She watched Dylan straddle her again, then lift Merritt's legs and sink down and move herself against the outside part of the vibrator.

"I thought scissoring was a myth," Merritt joked, her laugh cut off by a moan as Dylan ground her hips down, pressing the vibrator deeper.

"I'd love to fuck you with a strap, but riding you like this is the next best thing," Dylan whispered in her ear, her breath hot.

Merritt caught Dylan's mouth in a deep kiss, her hands and a leg wrapped around Dylan to hold their bodies together, sweat-soaked skin sliding against sweat-soaked skin.

The pressure in her lower belly started to tighten, her body tingling with the beginnings of a shattering orgasm.

All control she'd ever had snapped in an instant, and Dylan's name fell from her lips over and over. How many times had she said it? Dozens. *Dylan. Dylan. Dylan.* A question, an answer, a promise.

She lost track of time until Dylan's hips slowed over hers, letting her breathe as Dylan's face came back into focus, both of their hair wild and messy from fingers and sweat. Tremors shook her body, and she reached down to remove the vibrator, tossing it onto a napkin on the coffee table for future cleaning. Dylan's knuckles gently stroked her cheek, and she smiled up at the woman looking down at her, eyes searching.

That look felt a lot like love, and Merritt clamped down on the urge to say it just yet, but she lifted her mouth to press a gentle kiss to Dylan's lips in response.

"Merry Christmas to me," Merritt joked, already feeling sore and blissed out.

A lopsided smile appeared on Dylan's face. "Baby, we're just getting started."

MERRITT AWOKE TO SOFT, warm kisses on the back of her neck, making her nipples peak and tighten and goosebumps rise over her arms and shoulders. She reached back, tangling her fingers in Dylan's hair and scratching her scalp gently.

"Good morning," Dylan said.

"G'morning," Merritt mumbled. "You're up early."

"I brought you coffee," Dylan said.

"You're my hero," Merritt said, opening her eyes and smiling up at Dylan, who sat back to prop herself against the headboard. She pushed herself up on her elbows, stretching her neck. Sometime in the evening, they'd made it to the bed. She must have slept oddly, too exhausted from the satisfac-

tion of Dylan's tongue between her thighs and the reciproca-
tion of pleasure to be bothered with things like pillows or,
apparently, proper shoulder positioning. "We should really
ask Rebekah if we can get that king size bed back," she
groaned.

Dylan didn't answer, but simply pressed her lips together.

"Hey, we can stay with the twin size if you prefer," Merritt
said, awkwardly laughing to try to lighten the heavy mood
that had settled around them.

Dylan took a deep breath in through her nose. "You're
leaving today," she said finally.

"What day is it?" Merritt asked, having completely lost
track of dates.

"Mr. Vanlaningham has some kind of work emergency, so
you're all heading back before the New Year," Dylan said
quickly, staring straight ahead.

Dread pooled in Merritt's stomach. So soon? She'd thought
they had at least another five days together, and now they
had none? "Says who?"

And after? What happened when she walked out that
door?

"Says Mr. Vanlaningham this morning when I went to get
us the good coffee from the espresso machine," Dylan said
flatly.

Merritt sat up. "Are you mad at me right now? What's
with this tone?"

"I'm sorry, I'm just really disappointed, and I'm trying not
to cry," Dylan said, scowling.

"At least you're not crying in a room full of strangers
thinking you're being proposed to," Merritt said with a laugh
and shake of her head.

Dylan looked sideways at her, and Merritt could see that
her eyes were brimmed with tears. "Are we making jokes
right now?"

Dylan's poutiness made Merritt realize that she was

dreading goodbye just as much as Merritt was. After the past year, it was hard for her to take a leap of faith and trust Dylan, but now she knew that Dylan hadn't completely forgotten about her. And now she had to make sure that Dylan knew she wouldn't be forgotten, too. "Hey," Merritt said, setting her coffee on the bedside table and moving Dylan's to the same spot. She climbed into Dylan's lap, straddling her hips. Her hands cupped Dylan's cheeks. "We just have to deal with what's next a little sooner."

Dylan's hands rested on Merritt's hips as she nodded, sniffling. Dylan leaned forward, burying her head in Merritt's shoulder. "I just got you back. I don't want to lose you again."

Merritt wiped at Dylan's eyes and she couldn't help but smile with tenderness. Her ability to care for others overrode her own disappointment, and that wasn't necessarily a bad thing in this moment. "It's going to be okay. As long as you don't wait a month to text me, I *probably* won't block you again." Dylan blinked once, twice. Apparently that joke hadn't landed right. Merritt cleared her throat, adding, "We won't fuck this up."

"But like, is this going to be a long distance thing? I—"

Merritt leaned forward and pressed a gentle kiss to the corner of Dylan's mouth. "We don't have to figure out the details yet. We'll make it up as we go."

"Excuse me, but when did you turn into the rational one here?" Dylan asked, the first tiny quirk of a smile at the edge of her mouth.

"I've always been the rational one here," Merritt said.

"You are so ridiculous," Dylan said, rising up to flip Merritt backwards to lie down as she climbed on top of her, leaning on her elbows as Merritt laughed and protested beneath her. She sniffled and wiped at one of her teary eyes. "Maybe instead of planning, we could leave with a reminder of what we'll be missing."

"You do love a good distraction from the future," Merritt

teased, pressing a soft kiss to her throat, her hips pushing up into Dylan's thigh.

"Don't tell me you disagree with the plan," Dylan said, dipping her head to catch Merritt's mouth with hers.

"Have to leave you with something to remember me by, I suppose," Merritt said, wrapping her arms tighter around Dylan's neck.

CHAPTER 12

DYLAN

Was this a bad idea? Maybe.

But this was the only way she could make sure. She had to be sure.

It had been a long few days without Merritt. Somehow it had felt more like months.

They'd parted on such good terms—Merritt had kissed her, said goodbye, and said she'd call. Dylan packed up her things and helped Rebekah tidy the house once the Vanlaninghams had left, and then she'd left, too. She'd returned to her apartment in Denver to find that her succulent plant was dead and she'd left something rotting in the fridge.

She'd texted Merritt a few times—blue iMessages, thank god—but Merritt hadn't responded. Not once. Dylan had tried to cool her jets, recognizing that Merritt was traveling with a child and probably didn't have a lot of down time to sit around and text. Maybe she'd let Dylan know once she landed.

When the evening went by without a word from Merritt, Dylan started trying to stalk her on social media, but somehow Merritt was both absent from Facebook and didn't accept messages on her private Instagram. She hadn't known that was even an option.

She'd slept poorly that night, checking her phone every few minutes to see if Merritt had responded.

...Had Merritt ghosted her?

After everything that had gone down, had Merritt really thought that silence was the best way forward? Dylan now understood why Merritt had simply blocked her number early on—the waiting was awful.

An entire day passed, then another, without word from Merritt. She texted a few times each day to make sure she wasn't blocked, but every message went through with a blue bubble.

By the third day, she felt like she was losing touch with reality. Had everything they'd gone through over the past few weeks been a casual fling? Had she really read the situation so wrong to think that they'd have a future together?

This felt different than the last year of waiting for Merritt. She'd known what went wrong with the cowardly timing last year, but this year... She refused to believe that Merritt would just throw away her heart like that.

That was when the plan went a little rogue. It was a little creepy, but she looked through Merritt's followers on Instagram until she found her best friends Kylie and Ezra. Ezra was easy to find—they had a public profile and tons of followers, but Kylie was more private. Maybe she'd been the one to lock down Merritt's profile on the same level of secrecy as 2017 Taylor Swift.

Dylan typed up a message and included them both. Shooting her shot widely felt like it was more likely to be successful. "Hey, my name's Dylan, and I haven't been able to get ahold of Merritt for a few days. Just want to make sure she's okay, if you could pass along that I've been trying to get in touch with her."

Ezra responded almost immediately. "Merritt told us she never wants to talk to you ever again."

Dylan's heart sank.

Kylie's message came through soon after. "THEY'RE JOKING. They're joking. Oh my god, Ezra, Merritt is going to kill you for that."

Confused, Dylan blinked as she stared down at the phone.

Kylie was typing another message when Ezra sent, "Fine. She's just a hot mess express."

"She left her phone in Colorado, and the company sent the replacement *back* to Colorado instead of Westchester and Rebekah is out of town. She's been at the Apple and Verizon stores like six times in the past three days," Kylie explained.

"Why didn't she just message me on social media?" Dylan wrote.

"She doesn't use social media. She's like a caveperson," Ezra wrote. "She hasn't posted on Insta in like, four years. I bet she doesn't even remember it exists."

That was kind of cute and terribly out of touch. The uneasiness in Dylan's chest began to loosen.

"I have an idea," Ezra wrote. "How mobile are you? And do you have plans tomorrow?"

And that was how Dylan ended up in a taxi in Queens on New Year's Eve. It was snowing and the cab driver was driving like he was in a secret one-man race to hit 60 mph between each and every stop light. Dylan white knuckled the door handle, praying she wouldn't die before she arrived. The past few days had been a whirlwind of travel and planning, but she was here, and she was damn well going to make sure she didn't miss out on the chance she was taking.

Dylan loved a risk, but this felt terrifying beyond measure. She'd lived her entire life flying by the seat of her pants, but this? Going in blind? Her hands shook from nerves. She'd spent the entire plane ride to JFK trying not to throw up.

Ezra and Kylie assured her it was a good idea, but what if they were wrong?

Before she had any more time to panic, the driver stopped in front of what looked like a small house. She swiped her card and climbed out of the car, thankful to be on solid ground again. That was, until she took another step and slipped, falling flat on her back in the middle of the sidewalk.

The taxi drove off.

She had no other choice but to just lie there and die, she was fairly certain. She could move all of her limbs, but now she was covered in snow, and she'd taken such care to make her hair look good, and—

"Dylan?" A familiar face appeared in the sky, standing over her. Merritt's dark curls contrasted against the falling snow.

"Hey," Dylan said, nervous laughter bubbling up in her chest. She tried to push herself up, but was shoved backwards as Merritt practically tackled her back down.

"Oh my god, I've been so worried that you'd think I was the biggest asshole on earth," Merritt said, clinging to her.

Dylan smoothed back her hair, then realized with a start that Merritt wasn't wearing a coat. "Why are you in just a sweater?"

"I saw you get out of the taxi, then fall, from the front window and thought my mind was playing tricks on me, so I came out to check," Merritt explained hastily through frantic kisses pressed to Dylan's lips. "Anyways, listen, I wasn't ghosting. I lost my phone, so—"

"I know, babe," Dylan said, wrapping her coat around Merritt as best she could. "It's okay."

"You're not mad?"

"Consider us even," Dylan joked, kissing Merritt's face. She reached in her bag and pulled out the phone that had been mistakenly sent to the holiday house in Snowy Springs. Dylan had driven back to get it—Rebekah hadn't even *tried* to hide her delight as Dylan laid out the plan to take it to her in New York. "But let's not make it a habit."

Merritt squealed at the sight of the phone, but instead of reaching for it, she just clung to Dylan. The snow was falling silently all around, muffling the sounds of Astoria to where the only thing Dylan could hear was their kisses and laughter, their breath fogging the air. She became half-aware of the sounds of the party coming from Ezra's apartment, and tried not to look at the front window filled with grinning faces staring at them.

"Wait, why—*how* are you here?" Merritt asked.

"You think I'd miss kissing my girlfriend at midnight on New Year's?" Dylan scoffed, pretending to be affronted by the question.

"Your girlfriend, huh?" Merritt repeated, then shivered. "I see you're still feeling confident even after I ghosted you."

"Let's go inside and discuss that over a glass of wine," Dylan said, moving to stand on the slippery walkway. Merritt took her hand, and her cheeks ached from smiling. "Lead the way."

EPILOGUE

MERRITT

ALMOST ONE YEAR LATER

Merritt rubbed her temples, steps echoing down the hallway as her classmates filed out of the room. Psychological Research in Infancy was a rough course to have so late in the afternoon—she was both mentally exhausted and brimming with potential ideas, which always made her want to fall asleep the second she got home. Although, with the December sun setting so early, it might as well have been midnight. She yawned as she pushed open the doors to the street, the cold winter air stinging her cheeks.

Something about New York winters just sank into her bones—deeply cold, like she'd never be warm again. She daydreamed about a bath that evening, in Dylan's apartment. It was her first Christmas that she wouldn't be spending in Snowy Springs, and she didn't know why that made her feel a tiny bit sad. At least Christmas in New York was proving to be beautiful, from the snowflake pattern projected onto the sides of major buildings to the garlands and shining decorations that seemed to don every available surface.

A wolf whistle caught her attention and she looked around as she hugged her coat collar closer to her neck, spotting a woman leaning against a light post, looking effortlessly cool wearing a leather jacket, Wayfarers, and a smirk. *Dylan.*

Her stomach flipped, excitement and giddiness swirling inside even after months of seeing Dylan every day. She adjusted her tote bag on her arm and reached forward, holding the collar of Dylan's leather jacket as she rose up on her tip-toes to press a soft kiss to her lips. She was not even slightly embarrassed about the loved-up PDA, even as her classmates walked past and said goodbye to her.

"I brought you a snack," Dylan said, pressing her forehead to Merritt's as she reached into her pocket. "I know how the weird timing of this class makes it so you don't eat a proper lunch."

Merritt smiled, her cheeks aching with what felt like the millionth smile since Dylan had moved to New York City four months ago. She glanced down at the wrapped deli sandwich in Dylan's hand and squealed in delight. "For me?"

"Gotta keep my girl good and fed so she has the energy for what's to come later tonight," Dylan teased, giving Merritt's ass a light smack through her jeans.

Merritt shooed her hand away, her eyes widening as she looked up and down the street to check if anyone she knew—especially one of her professors—had seen them, but the cobblestone street outside of Kimball Hall seemed rather empty at the late hour.

"And what's to come later tonight?" Merritt smirked.

Dylan winked conspicuously, her dimple popping on her cheek. "Both of us, hopefully."

Merritt snorted, peeling back the white paper of the caprese sandwich from her favorite deli. "You're ridiculous."

"But before that, we've got company," Dylan said.

Merritt tilted her head. "What?"

"Remember? Julia and Huxley are coming over for dinner?" Dylan reminded her, eyebrows raised.

Merritt swallowed, cringing. "Fuck, I forgot."

"I didn't," Dylan said with a soft smile. "Dinner's all ready, just needs to go in the oven." She held out her elbow for Merritt to loop her arm through. They walked through Washington Square Park and hopped on the subway toward Dylan's Chelsea apartment, where Merritt spent most of her time anyway. She was on a student budget again, and although she had a solid savings account, most of that went toward basic living expenses.

Dylan, however, had become the right hand woman of Michaela Davis, currently one of the foodie scene's favorite chefs, famous for her innovative restaurant The Lighthouse. Julia had asked around her friend-group for Dylan, and Michaela had jumped at the chance to take Dylan under her wing. These days, with school and work, the few and far between moments they had together were extra special. Merritt hugged Dylan tighter to her side, asking about her day as they maneuvered their way along the subway stairs, platform, and train, hurrying only to stay warm.

"Are you excited to see Huxley again? It's been what... two weeks?" Dylan asked as they walked up the stairs and back onto the freezing street.

Merritt nodded, her mouth stuffed with the other half of the sandwich she'd unwrapped the second they'd walked back above ground. "Free weekth," she said, and Dylan watched her for a moment before parsing out that she had tried to say three weeks.

She missed Huxley terribly, but he was blossoming with his newfound independence and extra time spent with Julia and Kellen. The Vanlaninghams had hired a part-time nanny to make sure he got home from school okay, but the majority of the time he was with his parents. They'd both been traveling recently, and Merritt had stayed the weekend at the house to hang out with Huxley. It was nice to be back, but she was also grateful that it was temporary. Being back in Bronxville felt so lifeless after spending so much time in the city, and although her place of residence was technically in Ezra's Astoria guest bedroom, she felt more like Dylan's apartment was her real home each and every day.

She scarfed the rest of the sandwich as they walked past the doorman and paused in the elevator. As soon as Dylan hit the 9th floor button and the doors closed, she ran a hand through her hair and kicked the toe of her boot on the floor. Nervous energy rolled off of her in waves. Merritt eyed her.

"What's wrong?" she asked, struggling with the zipper of her coat.

Dylan snorted in amusement and reached forward, helping her put the zipper back on its track so that it could release the stranglehold it had on her body. "Nothing is wrong."

Merritt looked Dylan up and down for the first time since walking out of Kimball Hall. "You look really nice tonight."

Dylan's mouth quirked up in a smile. "Thanks. You do, too."

"Yeah, but you look... extra nice," Merritt said, noting Dylan's nice boots and button down. Did she have pomade in her hair? Since when did she start dressing up for Julia and Huxley?

Dylan licked her lips, biting the bottom one as the elevator doors opened and they walked into the hallway. Rosemary and a host of spices hit her, and she inhaled deeply. "Someone's dinner smells good." Her stomach rumbled loudly in agreement.

"You *just* ate a sandwich," Dylan teased as she fidgeted with her keys. She dropped them, and Merritt noticed her hands were shaking when she knelt to pick them up.

And then she stayed kneeling on one leg, looking up at

Merritt. She reached into her pocket, fumbling with something.

Merritt gasped, taking a step backward. "Oh my god," she said, trying to assess the situation even though her mind was racing a mile a minute. "Are you..."

Dylan looked around quickly. "What? No. I dropped my keys."

"You're not proposing right now?" Merritt said, pointing down to where Dylan was still kneeling on the ground. "Because you look nice and you got me a sandwich and now you're kneeling and—"

"—I am not proposing to you in a hallway," Dylan said, laughing. She shook her head, standing up and brushing off the front of her pants. "I dropped my keys."

Merritt didn't want to personally investigate why she felt slightly disappointed. Her phone dinged, startling her, and she looked from Dylan to the ground where she had just been kneeling.

"Who's texting you? Is it Mrs. Vanlaningham?" Dylan asked, taking just about one million years to put her key in the door.

Merritt took her phone out of her pocket and glanced at the screen, raising a skeptical eyebrow when she saw that the text was from Dylan. "You're texting me right now?"

Dylan paused, turning to look at her.

"Are you *texting* me a proposal—"

"Oh my god, Merritt, just look at the text."

Merritt swiped at her phone screen to open the message.

Will you move in with me?

Her hand came to her lips as her mouth dropped open in surprise. "Really?"

Dylan nodded.

"Like girlfriends who live together? Officially?" Merritt felt the need to clarify.

"Uh, yeah. Exactly like that. I mean, you spend most

nights here, and it seems a waste of money to keep paying for a room you barely use at Ezra's, and, you know. We'd be able to spend more time together with our crazy schedules, even if it's just for a few hours after the restaurant closes and before you run off to the lab. But no pressure. Just think about it. You don't have to answer just yet," Dylan said quickly, turning her key in the lock.

Merritt's thumbs flew across the screen and Dylan's phone buzzed. She paused, pulling her phone out of her pocket, and looked at the screen.

Hey, roomie.

Dylan smiled, her cheeks flushed. She leaned in to hold a finger under Merritt's chin, tipping her head back to steal a soft kiss. "That's a yes?"

"Yes," Merritt said and Dylan enveloped her in a hug.

"I love you," Dylan said, kissing the tip of her nose.

"I love you," Merritt said, the warmth of that statement never failing to amaze her. "Now, can we please get inside and stop giving all of the neighbors a free show?"

Dylan chuckled, taking the key out of the lock and handing it to her. "I suppose, but you know Mrs. Linkowski is definitely enjoying the view."

Merritt stepped inside the apartment after Dylan, then heard Dylan announce, "She said yes!" as she flipped on the lights. They were greeted with cheers, and Merritt watched as Ezra, Kylie, Julia, and Huxley jumped into the front hallway with party horns and laughter.

A laugh bubbled up in Merritt's throat as she hurried to hug everyone while they congratulated the pair on *finally* and *officially* U-Hauling. The group moved into the living room and Huxley demanded that they explain why it was called U-Hauling when lesbians moved in together. Judging by the silence of the group, no one was jumping to be the one to explain.

"It's just a funny phrase," Merritt assured him as he leaned against her side.

Kylie poured Merritt and Dylan a pair of cocktails, and Dylan wrapped an arm around Merritt's waist, raising her glass in a toast. "To the homes we find in one another."

The group raised their glasses in agreement, and Merritt looked up at Dylan, tears welling in her eyes. She'd never known home could be a person as much as a place, and she felt so lucky to have finally found a love and a home she had imagined only existed in fairy tales, and to be surrounded by a family she'd always longed for.

"Now, I think it's time for a Mario Kart rematch before dinner," Ezra said, clapping their hands and looking down at Huxley, who agreed with excitement.

"You're going down," Huxley teased, and they raced to the couch.

"Mrs. Vanlaningham, would you like to help me with the salad?" Dylan asked, kissing the top of Merritt's head and stepping away into the kitchen.

"Please, it's Julia, for the hundredth time, Dylan."

"Who needs another drink?" Kylie offered, the glass of the liquor bottles clinking as she reached into the bar cart for the whiskey.

Merritt paused, looking around at the bustling room, warm and filled with people she loved. She felt whole, and home, and excited for whatever new adventures were to come.

The End

Celebrate the holidays together with your favorite authors, with the Tis the Season Holiday Collection: nine sweet and tropey Christmas romance novellas to bring light and life this holiday season.

Check out the full collection at **lilyseabrooke.com/tis-the-season**, cozy up by the fire, and enjoy a sweet Christmas celebration, from all of us.

Happy holidays!

ACKNOWLEDGMENTS

First of all, thank you to YOU, dear reader, for continuing to support me and these little worlds I make up in my brain. This is all because of you and I am eternally grateful.

Major shoutout to my wife who I've watched grow into an amazing parent this year. Last Christmas was wild, maybe this year let's try boring.

To my editor, Lemon, thank you for befriending me on LiveJournal in 2006 and thank you for continuing to be an awesome person. Your insight and eagle-eye took this book to the next level.

And finally, to the family I've found throughout the years who have become my home. We're a weird bunch, but I love us.

ABOUT THE AUTHOR

Bryce Oakley is a Goldie-award winning author of sapphic romantic comedies and self-proclaimed pepperoni pizza connoisseur. She lives in Colorado with her partner, daughter, and a small herd of animals.